D0526283

HELLO FRIEND
WE MISSED YOU

Windsor and Maidenhead
9580000156033

HELLO FRIEND
WE MISSED YOU

Richard Owain Roberts

PARTHIAN

Parthian, Cardigan SA43 1ED
www.parthianbooks.com
First published in 2020
© Richard Owain Roberts 2020
ISBN 978-1-912681-49-5 paperback
ISBN 978-1-912681-93-8 ebook
Editor: Susie Wildsmith
Cover design by Emily Courdelle
Typeset by Elaine Sharples
Printed and bound by 4edge Limited, UK
Published with the financial support of the Books Council of Wales
British Library Cataloguing in Publication Data
A cataloguing record for this book is available from the British Library.

For Amy

Music To Crash To

Looking through the small oval window, deciphering only vague traces of geography and infrastructure through the clouds, Hill blinks slowly. Turning, he looks towards the pilots, two calm men silently staring ahead, occasionally pressing buttons on the dashboard. Hill touches his iPhone, opening then closing a free backgammon app, opening then closing a free solitaire app, opening then closing a free draughts app. Hill touches his iPhone and puts Ambient Sounds: Rain in a Barrel on repeat.

Thank you rain, thank you barrel, Hill thinks.

Hill looks towards a South American couple sitting opposite him. The woman, her loose, dark brown hair streaked with silver, is pointing a GoPro at the window, recording. The man, wearing a faded college sweater, black jeans, and scuffed multi-coloured Nikes, places his hands around the woman's neck, the woman playing along and flopping her tongue out, conveying *dead! you got me!* as she holds the GoPro in position, still recording, still documenting.

Hill looks away, touches his iPhone and puts Seinwave 2000 by Abelaard on repeat.

Hill looks back towards the couple, now pointing at the folksy illustrations of Celtic burial mounds and aspirational sea salt branding that cover one side of an expanded tourist pamphlet.

'Guide To Anglesey *Arweiniad i Ynys Môn*', Hill thinks.

Hill listens as they repeat *Bear Grylls Island Rib Ride* back to each other over and over, grinning.

Hill turns up the volume on his iPhone, looks straight ahead and closes his eyes.

The aeroplane cabin rattles violently for a moment, and then continuously for a sustained period. Hill opens his eyes and watches the South Americans laughing as they struggle to pour water from a bottle of Brecon Carreg into a silver hipflask without it spilling on the grubby metal floor.

Happy maniacs, Hill thinks.

Hill looks around the cabin; two middle-aged women wearing charcoal business suits are talking and looking at a tablet, two middle-aged men wearing white shirts tucked into chino shorts are talking and looking at a tablet, a woman in her twenties is gripping her armrest, her nails digging into the worn, faded material as she maintains a calm and stoic facial expression.

Like Lucy, Hill thinks.

Hill un-mutes the volume on his iPhone and looks ahead.

Hill becomes conscious of the aeroplane tilting, shuddering, then beginning to make its descent.

Seinwave 2000 starts playing again.

How many times, Hill thinks.

Music to crash to, Hill thinks.

Survival odds, Hill thinks.

It's okay, Hill thinks.

Hill looks ahead and shuts his eyes.

Drug cat

The taxi driver pulls up at the side of the road. The driveway is half a kilometre long, but Roger only arranged to pay up to the gate and Hill has no money on him.

'Classic Roger', Hill thinks.

Hill looks at the wrought iron gates, open and pressed back against the high stone wall, only partially visible amongst the overrunning ivy and nettle bushes. He turns around and looks in the direction of the taxi, the driver is adjusting his earpiece, speaking, laughing.

Did I talk enough on the journey, Hill thinks.

Didn't speak at all, Hill thinks.

Hill feels regret for not having brought the suitcase with wheels. He doesn't know what is making the suitcase so heavy; all that he can remember packing is socks, pants, one pair of jeans, and a couple of T-shirts. He made the conscious choice to leave his laptop at home. Hill told Ed he would be uncontactable for most of the time he was on the island, and wasn't sure how long that would be; he explained that Roger was very ill, mentally unstable, pathetically insistent on him staying at the house.

Hill stands at the wrought iron gate, suitcase in one hand and cat carrier in the other. The taxi pulls away into the distance and towards the A-road that runs uninterrupted from one end of the island to the other.

Is Dave awake, Hill thinks.

Resting the suitcase on the ground, Hill holds the cat carrier in both hands and lifts it up to eye level. Peering through the metal grill he looks at Dave, curled up and still feeling the sleeper.

Drug cat, Hill thinks.

Hill lowers the pet carrier to the floor and picks it up by the handle. He looks at the suitcase and sighs.

The trees and woodland that surround the driveway look exactly the same as they did when Hill lived there. Towards the edges of the driveway the grass is neatly kept, gradually becoming wilder until the denseness of the bushes and trees is only broken by a hacked pathway or old tree trunk. Hill listens to the wind and looks at the leaves on the large, old trees.

Objectively beautiful, Hill thinks.

Did I ever appreciate this, Hill thinks.

Hill picks up the suitcase and tries to work a comfortable way of slinging it over his shoulder. This is worse. Hill keeps trying until he feels the sharp edge of the small Yale lock scratch above his neckline. He throws the suitcase to the floor.

Nope, Hill thinks.

Nope, Hill thinks.

Nope, Hill thinks.

Standing still for a moment, he closes his eyes and listens for the sound of waves; beyond the driveway, beyond the house, beyond the front lawn, beyond the rocky path but still there, still existing.

Sailing lessons hell, Hill thinks.

Ambient waves sleep app hell, Hill thinks.

He picks the pet carrier up and begins walking down the driveway, a slow, warm line of blood and sweat creeping down his back.

Luke's plastic face

Roger emailed six months ago to explain that the clock tower was being converted into a holiday let. He had become more interested in financial matters over the last few years, often emailing Hill links to Forbes.com articles and detailing the performance of his small portfolio of shares. He had suggested that Hill should think about a postgraduate business qualification, that Hill needed to monetise, that Money Is The Freedom That Powers Us Forwards™. Hill hadn't responded to the clock tower email and refused to discuss it when he spoke to Roger on the phone. Roger had explained that it would make them a lot of money, money that Hill could use if he wanted.

Shut up, Roger, Hill thinks.

So quiet here, Hill thinks.

Hill steps off the driveway and walks into the woodland. He thinks about his mother and how she used to watch him climb trees and play with his Star Wars figures.

Don't be afraid, Hill, higher—

She encouraged him to plot out original stories rather than imitate the films; Darth Vader setting up a treetop cafe with Chewbacca, Luke spending his life alone, living in a rose bush that overlooked the entire universe. To signify the passing of time, Hill drew a moustache on Luke's plastic face that developed into a goatee that developed into a full Russian beard.

You're so thoughtful, you get that from me—

She used the clock tower to store her old clothes, fancy dress costumes, all her school teaching resources. She spent time in there sorting through things with Hill, telling him stories about her father's life as an opera singer, their life in the house, the clock tower, the family holidays they went on. Until her late teens, Hill's mother was the only person in her school to have flown in an aeroplane.

For us, it was just normality—

Roger was afraid of flying, and every summer Hill and his mother travelled abroad for three or four weeks without him. Sometimes during the winter they would sit together in the clock tower and look through Polaroids of their holidays:

A woman and a boy drinking red wine, a woman and a boy feeding stray cats, a woman and a boy playing Snap. A woman and a man eating Greek salad, a woman and a boy eating Greek salad, a woman and a man drinking red wine, a woman and a boy drinking red wine. A woman and a boy laughing, a woman and a boy sitting quietly, reading. A woman, a man, and a boy standing next to a fishing boat, a woman, a man, and a boy eating baklava in a restaurant. A woman and a boy wearing matching striped T-shirts, a woman and a boy staring directly into camera, their tongues sticking out, a woman and a boy staring directly into camera, expressionless and calm.

So gorgeous, Hill, in these moments—

Hill felt it was important to see the clock tower first, feel emotional, and then react calmly when Roger would later insist on him going to inspect the revamped building.

'Elegant bi-fold solutions for that classic contemporary finish', Hill thinks.

Bi-fold doors in every single room, in every single wall, Hill thinks.

Bi-fold Sarah Beeny, bi-fold Kirstie Allsopp, Hill thinks.

Hill looks back towards the driveway momentarily, but turns and keeps walking deeper into the woodland until he joins a long unmaintained path that leads to the clock tower.

***

Hill opens the moss-covered gate and stands in front of the clock tower. It is exactly as he remembered it, the stone walls green and damp in patches around the door and the ground floor windows, the clock dial frozen and rusted. He puts the pet carrier down, walks up to the building and runs his hands over the rotting wooden window frames.

Feels okay, Hill thinks.

Feel okay, Hill thinks.

Well, you saw the clip

Hill stands in front of the back door to the house. He turns around and looks at the red Peugeot 205 parked next to Roger's ancient Volvo estate. The Peugeot has mismatched replacement bodywork and a large opaque sticker that reads GTI on the rear window.

'Paul Walker Never Forget', Hill thinks.

The back door would have been intended as a staff entrance when the house was built in the latter half of the eighteenth century; wide, low, the panelled oak now painted fern green with heavy, black door furniture Hill's mother bought from a local auction house. Hill looks down and sees a doormat with 'Seize Opportunity' written on it in a large red font.

Roger, Hill thinks.

Reaching into his pocket for a key, Hill notices one already in the lock. He sighs, turns the large door handle, and walks inside.

The utility room is essentially a long corridor with a strip of reclaimed worktop running on one wall from the back door up to the kitchen door. Underneath the worktop are old boots, Roger's umbrella reserves, stacks of roughly chopped logs. Walking up the corridor towards the kitchen, Hill feels his stomach twist and cramp. He turns to face the wall and places the pet carrier on the worktop, pressing his face against the metal grid.

Let me in, Hill thinks.

Hill!

Hill pulls back from the pet carrier and looks towards the woman standing in the kitchen doorway. She is wearing an oversized navy cable-knit sweater, grey skinny jeans, barefoot. A brindle boxer is pushing its head between her thighs, panting, struggling to get out of the kitchen.

Are you Roger's carer? Hill says.

Um, yes? Trudy, she says. I was expecting you earlier, Hill.

They lost my suitcase, Hill says.

I thought that flight was carry-on only? Trudy says.

Is that your dog? Hill says, pointing at the boxer, a thin line of drool now hanging from its mouth.

Yeah! Well, Roger loves him too, so, Trudy says.

Hill shrugs his shoulders.

It's not problematic him being here is it? Trudy says, looking down at the dog. I mean, it is Roger's house.

'Problematic', Hill thinks.

'Roger's house', Hill thinks.

***

Hill looks around the kitchen. The Aga is filthy, dry pasta sauce crusted on top of the hobs, spilling over onto the adjacent work surface. There is a Hudl on the table, a stack of Financial Times in the corner, and a half-empty bottle of Evian next to the large butler sink. The room smells of burnt saucepans and burning vegetables.

Yeah, I'm pretty big into cooking these days, Trudy says. I found this recipe, totally incredible, for a Turkish ratatouille. Roger loves it, has no idea it's vegan. He wants it every day. So compulsive. Sorry, I didn't ask – how was the flight?

Fine, Hill says, sitting down at the table. He watches as Trudy picks up a wooden spoon from the kitchen worktop, lick it clean, and use it to stir the ratatouille.

Are you a qualified carer? Hill says.

I met Roger in the Co-op, Trudy says. Isn't that how everyone gets these jobs?

Trudy picks up her phone from the worktop, holding it above her head for signal as she walks over towards the window where she then stands, her back turned to Hill.

I have a voicemail but no reception to listen to it, Trudy says. Is that somehow profound?

Roger said that you were cutting your hours? Hill says.

I have more PhD stuff to deal with now, Trudy says. Basically you'll be doing the Co-op run twice a week.

Is there a list, I won't be able to do it from memory, Hill says. I mean I don't know what he likes. He emailed me an article about avocados a few months ago, something 'insane sounding' maybe.

That's funny, Trudy says. You, right now, you're literally Roger. Somehow. I don't know, you look nothing like him, but. Yeah. I saw a clip from your ... film? Something you'd emailed Roger. I'd like to ask you about it... Roger said it's a comedy?

Well, you saw the clip, Hill says.

Trudy stares at Hill and momentarily tilts her head to the side. She is tall, at least the same height as him, her hair shoulder length, a little greasy, blonde with prominent dark roots. Trudy nods and smiles, then holds her phone up above head height, tilting the screen away from the light. Hill watches as she moves onto tiptoes and touches the phone's screen.

Okay, I need to go now, Hill, Trudy says. I'll text you a shopping list; Roger gave me your number. I have to meet my, um... I'll be back for five, but it could be six or half six, conceivably seven. All this ratatouille needs is stirring. Maybe turn the heat up again in five minutes?

Trudy walks around Hill and picks up a pair of grey and black Berghaus walking boots from the radiator behind him.

God, Trudy says, inhaling. Problematic shoe situation.

Hill feels himself flush red.

Please don't be embarrassed for me, Hill, Trudy says. Anyway, maybe seven this evening or a bit later? Unless you could be on

Roger-Watch? He doesn't need it, but I like to stay over sometimes just in case. I don't know. Is that okay?

Yeah, that's fine, Hill says, making an awkward thumbs up gesture.

What, Hill thinks.

Okay, Hill, 'thumbs up', Trudy says.

Hill watches as Trudy squats down and tucks the laces down the side of each boot, the dog clumsily squeezing past her, barking as it runs down the corridor towards the back door. Picking up an unbranded backpack and a Co-op bag full of clothes, she calls out to the dog and shuts the kitchen door behind her.

'Thumbs up', Hill thinks.

There is a loud engine noise and the sound of gravel churning, then quiet. Hill looks inside the fridge, takes an unopened bottle of Brecon Carreg and places it on the worktop.

No bad thoughts, no thoughts at all, Hill thinks.

Hill picks up the bottle of Brecon Carreg and begins reading the label. He looks over to the washing machine and sees a grey sports bra and single lime green sock on the floor in front of it. He looks at a framed photo of Roger and the old family dog Jess standing on the Menai Bridge pier and tries to remember whether he took the photo. He holds his phone in front of the photograph and takes a burst of images, close-ups of the dog and the large military ship docked at the end of the pier. He moves away from the photo and takes an apple from the fruit bowl. He reads the label on the apple and places it back in the fruit bowl. He walks over to the Aga and stirs the ratatouille for a moment. He picks up the Hudl and looks at a pair of second-hand mom jeans for sale on the open Depop app.

Mom jeans, Hill thinks.

How would Trudy dance, Hill thinks.

What, Hill thinks.

Hill sits down on the floor, leans his back against the warm oven front and sets up a first to fifteen match against the Hudl backgammon app.

Photo 419 of 834

Hill sits on the Chesterfield in the study and opens Roger's MacBook. Unchecking 'remember me on this computer', Hill logs into Facebook and searches 'Trudy Dafis'.

Photos of Trudy:

Trudy at a house party.

Trudy at a house party.

Trudy on a Venezuelan beach.

Trudy on a Venezuelan beach.

Trudy at a house party.

Trudy at a house party.

Trudy 'deep' in a Peruvian jungle.

Trudy 'deep' in a Peruvian jungle.

Trudy at a house party.

Trudy at a house party.

Trudy standing with a ~70-year-old man at graduation, grinning.

Trudy standing with a ~70-year-old man at graduation, grinning.

Trudy at a house party.

Trudy at a house party.

Trudy at a house party.

Trudy at a house party.

Trudy at a house party.

In a photo numbered 419 of 834, Trudy is standing by a window overlooking the Menai Strait, staring back towards the island from the mainland. There are other people in the room, wearing Rip Curl T-shirts and board shorts, all piled onto a faded floral print sofa and looking at something out of the camera shot. Trudy is holding a can of Coors Light in one hand and a pair of large white sunglasses in the other. There is a blotchy redness around her eyes, like she might have been crying. Her hair is down, shoulder length, much lighter than it is now, and bleached maybe. Hill zooms in on the photo until Trudy's lips fill the screen. He feels uncomfortable and zooms out. He looks at the other people in the photo; they all seem so engaged and happy in this situation. One of them is holding a can of Coors Light and has a large wet patch on his trouser leg, his mouth wide open like he's screaming. Hill thinks about what they might be looking at. He looks back to Trudy. The photo is from two years ago. Hill thinks about two years ago. He was imagining living in LA with Lucy. He was drinking every day and feeling happy to know Ed and the other people in their friendship group. He was drinking every day and talking on Gmail chat with other independent filmmakers from around the world. He was drinking every day and talking on the phone with Roger at least twice a week, and even if it was mainly Roger doing the talking it felt okay, conceivably reconciliatory. Two years ago, Trudy was feeling sad in a house party and Hill was drinking every day and feeling happy.

Hill looks at the photo.

Hill clicks like.

Hill realises that he and Trudy aren't Facebook friends.

Hill realises that he and Trudy aren't real world friends.

Hill says fuck and clicks unlike.

Hill shuts the MacBook and thinks about photo 419 of 834.

TripAdvisor *** rated gastro pub

I don't really drink now, Hill says.

Is it okay if I drink? Trudy says. Oh, by the way, this is weird maybe, but did you like, and then unlike, a photo I was tagged in?

I can have one drink, Hill says.

Define success though

Hill and Trudy are sitting at the kitchen table drinking smoothies made with cinnamon, almond, oat milk, wheatgerm, cacao powder, and banana.

Hill is staring at his drink, watching separation occur, wishing he couldn't see this, wondering about Roger's hospital appointment and how much shit Roger was probably giving the consultant.

Is it deliberate? Trudy says. I mean … how do people usually respond to your silences? If Jack Black bought the rights to my film I'd—

Did I tell you that? Hill says, experiencing a creeping sense of devastation.

No, Roger did, Trudy says. In the Co-op. Within ten minutes of us meeting. He told me he always believed something like that would happen to you—

Nope, Hill says.

He said that you get your sense of humour from him—

Nope, Hill says.

Honestly, you don't seem that funny most of the time, Trudy says. But Roger is funny a lot of the time, so I trust his judgement.

I mean, Hill says. I can't–

What's the film about? Roger tried to explain, but I don't remember, or I don't think he explained it that well—

Are you still drunk? Hill says.

Are you?

I don't think I was drunk. I'm very disciplined with alcohol.

You were really drunk, Trudy says. You told me about your ex-wife, she sounds nice.

'Ex-wife', Hill thinks. 'Sounds'.

Hill feels sick.

Hill picks up his smoothie, looks at it, puts it back down on the table.

Thank you for this drink, Hill says. I can tell you 'about' 'Jack Black' if you want.

Yes! Trudy says. 'Sure!'

Jack Black bought a two-year option. We had a meeting—

In Hollywood?

Hill shakes his head. Please let me get this over with, he says.

21

Trudy nods and clicks the play button on an imaginary Dictaphone.

That's great. Okay, no—

Trudy mimes turning the Dictaphone off and putting it in the breast pocket of her shirt.

Jack Black bought a two-year option to remake the podcast, Hill says.

Can I listen to this podcast? Sorry!

To remake the podcast as a movie, Hill says.

Why would he do that?

It wasn't a real podcast, Hill says. It was a fake podcast that we came up with and filmed ourselves recording.

What was the podcast about?

It was a fake podcast, Hill says. You never really heard the podcast.

I can see this is *very Hill*. Very, very Hill, Trudy says.

Yep, Hill says.

The Secret Life of Podcasters Gone Wild—

Yep.

And you were in this? Trudy says. Talking? Acting?

Well, um. Sorry, I just want to finish this, Hill says. We had a Skype meeting in my studio and ... Jack said we were talented people with a brilliant concept and he wanted the world to appreciate it like he did. He was wearing circular, clear frames and a white polo neck. He didn't smile for the whole time he was talking to us, and afterwards we all felt confused and impressed somehow. Seems insane and sinister in hindsight. Then after two years of total silence, a few months ago someone from his production company emailed and said that he was as passionate as ever about the project and would be renewing the option for another two years. I mean, I, it's good, it's great.

Trudy takes a small sip from her smoothie and begins nodding her head.

I'm honestly about to cry, Trudy says. I'm definitely still drunk. I mean, define success though. Fuck it. Film another fake podcast. Film a real podcast. Film a fake real podcast about the filming of the fake podcast. Just do something about it you lazy bums.

We'll work on something, um, Hill says. Ed's busy. I need some time out, I think. Anyway, the Jack Black thing might still happen...

I want to hug you, you look so sad, Trudy says. You are successful. You have your own studio—

Studio apartment, Hill says.

Hill starts laughing and Trudy starts laughing. They are both crying a little.

Roger doesn't need picking up from the hospital for another hour, Trudy says. I could roll a really weak joint?

Trudy gets up from the table and leaves the kitchen. Hill listens as the upstairs floorboards creak directly above him. He can hear music coming from the bedroom Trudy uses for her overnight stays.

'Trudy's room', Hill thinks.

Hill looks at the smoothie and puts his hand around the tall glass. It still feels cold. Hill leans forward and lets his nose hover above, then briefly touch, the frothy top layer of smoothie.

Thank you for making this, Hill thinks.

Hill hears Trudy shouting down. He picks up the glass, drinks half, and takes it upstairs with him.

Email drafts written whilst listening to Classic FM 1:45-4:45AM

Dear Jack

Dear Jack!

Jack

Jack!

Hi Jack!

Hi Jack

I want to say thank you again for showing an interest in my work, that's an incredible compliment and something that keeps me in good spirits always. I must sound like a stuck record by now, but I mean it.

What films are you watching at the moment? I'm always keen to hear other people's recommendations. I think we have a similar aesthetic!

I was so enthusiastic to hear your plans for our project. It's a great feeling to know that we are on the same page with this – I always had television in mind by the way, even if perhaps everyone else (Ed) didn't see it that way. I'd love to be involved on some level with the production, perhaps I could send you a treatment? You must be incredibly busy with this and all of your other projects, but if you'd ever like to check anything or go over any details, I would be happy to answer any questions you might have.

Life is good for me. I'm taking a holiday at the moment and working on some new ideas. It feels really nice to be in a calm and creative environment (I imagine this is what LA is like?) I might be moving house soon, so if you need to send me anything it's best you do it via email only at this stage (I'll let you know when this changes). I loved Sex Tape, a really great cameo, probably the high point of the whole film. Perhaps you could have a supporting role in our project?

All the best, Hill

The banana car still somehow smells of banana

The cars in the adjacent lane start moving slowly towards the island. Hill looks at the vehicles in front of him, static, the queue stretching beyond the bridge and towards Bangor.

'Bangor University graduate Danny Boyle', Hill thinks.

Danny Boyle, my mother, Roger, Trudy, the list goes on, Hill thinks.

Hill puts the Volvo in neutral, lifts the handbrake, and turns the engine off. Uncle Robert shut the engine down at every red light and sometimes when travelling downhill. Uncle Robert ate banana after banana on car journeys to and from Hill and his cousins' swimming lessons, tossing the skins either in the small storage space in front of the gearstick or sometimes on the passenger seat. The car always smelt of banana. Uncle Robert sold the banana car to Roger. Twenty years later, Uncle Robert is dead and the banana car still somehow smells of banana.

Important banana legacy, Hill thinks.

Hill looks in the rear-view mirror. The man in the car behind him, a brown vintage Volkswagen, is nodding his head and moving his lips. Hill looks across to the right hand lane, now also gridlocked. Teenage boys with bouffant hair and tightly-shaped eyebrows run in single file on the pedestrian walkway, grimacing, weighed down by camouflage backpacks and black boots.

Call of Duty: Modern Poppy Aesthetic, Hill thinks.

Hill looks towards the water. It's late afternoon but still light, a motorboat tows a wakeboarder, riding and bouncing over the waves, at first with two hands and then with one. The wakeboarder wipes out and the boat slows down, turns side-on to the wakeboarder, and stops. Hill looks straight ahead and then leans forward and peers up towards the top of the bridge's central arch where two large gulls stand next to each other, looking in opposite directions, squawking.

Unsure if this is what bottleneck is, Hill thinks.

Hill feels a dull ache from somewhere inside his head and looks at the six pack of Coors Light on the passenger seat. He presses his hand on the side of the box. He can feel the chill of the cans through the thin cardboard packaging.

He looks ahead at the cars in front of him, stationary.

Hill opens the box and takes a can. He holds the can in front of his face and leans in towards it, the cold sensation numbing his forehead. He thinks about Uncle Robert, his cousins, bananas, swimming lessons with Hans, Hans' large red pectoral birthmark, front crawl, butterfly, breathing techniques, being dunked by Hans, the seven-and-a-half metre diving board, the ten-metre diving board, the feeling of hitting the water hands first, the feeling of hitting the water belly first, the feeling of Hans saying *gooood*, the feeling of Hans saying *nat gooood*, the loud changing room, the tired walk from the pool to the car park at the edge of the complex, the car journey home, Uncle Robert, his cousins, bananas—

Hill becomes conscious of car horns and looks ahead, the nearest car in front of him now on the other side of the central arch. Hill drops the Coors Light in his lap, turns the engine on, and puts the car into second.

***

Trudy's building is set back from the road. There is nothing on this road apart from trees and large houses behind high walls. Most of the houses have been converted into HMOs or student accommodation. The student accommodation is of an objectively high standard; the HMOs are of an objectively poor standard. There is something for everyone.

Hill parks the car and picks up the Coors Light from between his legs and puts it back in the box. A Ford, a Mazda, a Peugeot, and a Daewoo fill up the gravelled area to the side of Trudy's house.

Seems arbitrary how people choose, Hill thinks.

The building is a large four-storey Edwardian house, converted into flats some time in the 1980s. Hill looks up towards the third floor. The windows are single glazed and tired looking, only specks of white paint remaining on the wooden frames. He sees Trudy walk up to the window and awkwardly attempts to slide down his seat and out of view.

Ridiculous, Hill thinks.

Hill waits a moment and looks back up towards the window. Trudy is standing, staring out trance-like towards the strait, carefully mapping out a collection of small shapes with her index finger. She pauses momentarily, turns her back to the window, and walks out of view.

Hill checks his watch and opens the car door.

James Woods, what the hell

Is this actually from a school? Hill says. He sits on the small orange plastic chair, opens a can of Coors Light and passes it to Trudy.

I don't know, maybe, it was here when I moved in, Trudy says, leaning forward and taking the can. She's sitting on the futon, ordering loose paper into a green lever-arch file. Sorry, I'm nearly finished, she says. What do you think? I mean I know it's shitty, but I've only been here three months.

It's nice, seems like how I would imagine it, Hill says, looking at the original coving running around the edges of the ceiling. Three of the walls have been wood-chipped, the others are bulging and cracked from bad plastering work. The carpet is a dark magenta shade, cheap and industrial, but mostly covered by well-worn Persian rugs. To the side of the futon is a large floor-lamp, elaborately carved into the shape of an overhanging branch.

That's interesting, Hill says, pointing towards the lamp.

My friend made it, he's incredibly talented, probably too talented if you can imagine that?

Hill shrugs and takes a large swig from his Coors Light.

Trudy closes the lever-arch file and rests it on top of a small pile of books. She stands up and walks over towards the tall bay window at the other end of the room, motioning for Hill to follow.

Hill and Trudy stand in front of the window and look towards the strait. Do you want to know what I was doing when I was standing here before? Trudy says. When you were in the car, you dummy.

I... yeah, Hill says.

I was mapping out part of the Åland Islands' inner archipelago, Trudy says. So beautiful. Seems so disparate from our island experience. I don't know.

Hill looks at Trudy. Her finger, moving carefully, delicately, appearing somehow autonomous, maps out several unique island outlines, each one a trace of something real.

We should put a film on, Trudy says.

***

I can't believe we just watched that... truly problematic, Trudy says, laughing. She shuts her MacBook and leans over the side of the bed to turn the projector off. I'm going to roll a really weak joint, okay?

I'm surprised by how much I didn't hate it, Hill says. I mean, I thought it was really boring. James Woods, what the hell—

Exactly, James Woods what the hell, Trudy says. Do you find Maggie Gyllenhaal attractive?

Trudy gets up from the bed and walks into the kitchenette.

Hill looks at his watch. It is 02:30. His iPhone has been flashing with messages from Ed. If he looks at them he will feel compelled to answer. His finger moves over the BBC Sport app. If he looks at it he will feel compelled to engage with sports. His finger moves over the weather app.

Don't do it, Hill thinks.

Do you want to stay over? Trudy asks. She is wearing an oversized navy cable-knit sweater, black leggings, barefoot.

I, Hill says.

Might be 'a disaster', Hill thinks.

Hill remembers the last time he had sex. He remembers one of Lucy's friends from university talking to him in a bar six months after Lucy died. He remembers taking cocaine with her and talking confidently about Jack Black's aesthetic philosophy. He remembers her new build flat's tiny bedroom. He remembers her impatience at how long it took him to put a condom on. He remembers the seemingly ironic mouse ornaments on the shelf above the bed. He remembers pretending to come. He remembers the look of boredom on her face as they lay there afterwards, talking about a Jamie's that recently opened across the road from her building.

I haven't showered today, Hill says.

We should have a bath, Trudy says.

Hill and Trudy are lying on top of the duvet. Hill is naked, Trudy has put on a pair of bright green pants. Hill leans over the edge of the bed and picks up his phone to check the time then picks up a can of Coors Light and takes a small sip.

Patented Coors and booty taste, Hill thinks.

What time do you normally go to sleep? Hill says, looking over towards his phone.

Earlier, Trudy says. My bed at Roger's is nicer than this one. He bought me a memory foam, I think you have my old one.

Hill grits his teeth.

Unreal, Hill thinks.

Trudy leans over the edge of the bed and picks up her laptop, the glare of the open screen illuminating her stomach.

I met this French Canadian guy in Peru, Trudy says. He was really young, maybe seventeen, all he wanted to do was eat my butt. We should try and find him on Facebook.

Why would we do that? Hill says.

Less open tabs, more open hearts, Hill, Trudy says. She scans through the profiles of Vincents listed as living in Montreal. Maybe that wasn't his real name, she says. He said he was trying for a golf scholarship at an American university or something, so—

34

Nope, Hill thinks.

I need to be up early tomorrow, I'll go, Hill says, wiping his hands on the sheet and getting up from the bed.

What the fuck, Hill? Trudy says.

I need to take Roger to the hospital, seeing as you can't, Hill says. He picks up his clothes and walks with them into the bathroom, slamming the door behind him.

I'm sorry you're not the first person I've ever let be intimate with my bum, Hill, Trudy says.

Hill turns on the cold tap, cups his hands, and repeatedly splashes water around his mouth and chin. He can hear Trudy's voice in the other room and leaves the tap running whilst he dresses. Hill checks himself in the mirror again, turns the tap off, and shuts the bathroom door behind him.

Are you okay to drive? Trudy says.

Did you find Vincent? Hill says. Say hi from me.

Okay, that's fine, I will, Trudy says. Remember to pick up Roger's medication from the chemist tomorrow.

Hill stands and watches Trudy type.

Okay, great, Hill says.

Hill looks at his phone to check the time and walks over to the door and out onto the communal landing.

Sitting in his car, Hill feels faint, exhausted. The weed and the alcohol are still in his system and he senses feelings of depression and resentment.

Unsure what happened, Hill thinks.

He starts the engine and drives out of the car park and onto the main road. There are no other cars on the road, no other cars on the bridge, only a large Waitrose delivery truck that struggles to fit through the two-hundred-year-old arches. Hill looks at the speedometer, squints, then gives up.

Halfway to Roger's house, Hill becomes aware that he is losing consciousness. He pulls over in a lay-by and turns the car engine off. He looks at his iPhone and reads the messages from Ed.

Ed: Oi Tall Tree, are you with the carer

Ed: Have you had sex

Ed: Are you going to

Ed: Honestly I think you should, Sad Salmon

Ed: Maybe you're doing it now

Ed: Loose Leaf, I'll message tomorrow

Hill puts the iPhone down on the passenger seat, rests his head on the headrest, and closes his eyes. A man on the radio is talking about the weather, a woman on the radio is talking about Islamic State, a woman on the radio is talking about plastic, a man on the radio is talking about—

The animals must have proper agency

Hill watches as Trudy places copies of The Times, The Financial Times, and The Bangor & Anglesey Mail in a pile on the kitchen table. She looks at Hill and nods, smiling as she unpacks each paper and makes separate piles for the news, financial, and sports sections.

Jesus, Hill says.

Trudy's dog walks past Hill and towards the sink. He props himself up against the worktop, tilts his head and begins licking congealed gravy from Roger's evening hotplate.

Can you stop him, Hill says.

I think we should introduce Ralph and Dave-cat to each other today, Trudy says. I think it's time they met and accepted that they have to share this space. How have you been by the way?

Fine, thank you, Hill says. I don't understand what's happening. Ralph doesn't live here, he's your dog. You don't live here. Why can't he wait outside, or in your car? I mean, you're not even here for the basic hours Roger pays you for.

Hill looks at Trudy and she seems possibly hurt by this comment.

Should say something nice or make a joke, Hill thinks.

But I hate Roger, so it's all good, Hill says.

Trudy turns away from Hill and picks up a quarter-full bottle of Sherbourne Springs.

I'm joking, Hill says. I'm fucking joking.

Yeah. I suppose that works, Trudy says. She turns round to face Hill and takes a long drink from the bottle, staring at Hill the whole time, finishing the water, screwing the cap back on the bottle, placing the bottle down on the work surface, folding her arms across her chest.

Great, thank you. I'm glad you got that I was joking, Hill says. I still don't know why they have to meet—

Ralph and Dave will be coming into contact on a regular basis for as long as you stay here with your dad, Trudy says. It's his house, and he did say it was okay for Ralph to be here. I think we need to do this today, right now. I have to be at my PhD workshop in an hour, so I need Ralph to be here.

Okay, Hill says. I might have been busy–

I'm going to get Ralph, Trudy says. Go and find Dave and bring him into the kitchen.

Hill walks up the stairs and into his bedroom. The room has a queen-size bed, a bookshelf filled with A Level English set texts and study guides, a wide plastic clothes rail, and a small purple sink in the corner. Dave is asleep on the bed, his whiskers twitching. Hill picks him up and carries him down the stairs.

Dave, Dave, Dave, wake up, Hill says. I know this is fucked up but you need to meet Roger's carer's dog right now. I don't know, if you can make it obvious how much you hate him that would be really helpful for me. I literally rescued you, Dave. Please.

Hill stops outside the kitchen door. He can hear Trudy talking to Ralph. Hill nudges Dave a little. You hate this dog okay, he says.

Hill opens the kitchen door. Trudy has brought in a dog bed from the boot of her car and Ralph is lying down in it, his tail wagging.

The animals must have proper agency, Trudy says. She walks over to Hill and takes Dave. She carries Dave over to the dog basket, making purring sounds into his ears, and places him down next to Ralph. Dave climbs into the dog basket, on top of Ralph, and starts kneading his neck. Ralph begins making a low-level guttural dog noise, his tail still wagging, rhythmically, less manically than before.

This is a disaster, Hill says. He moves towards the dog basket but is blocked by Trudy.

They like each other, they're connected, Trudy says. I think they must have picked up on our desire to make this work.

I'm going for a shower, Hill says. If you're making a smoothie for Roger, please can you make enough for me, and if you're doing the cinnamon one, please can you try and make it with less cinnamon?

Trudy is taking photos of Dave and Ralph, now both asleep, sharing the dog basket.

I'll make sure there's not too much cinnamon, and also that there's enough for all of us, Trudy says, raising her middle finger and aiming it in Hill's direction. Hey look, Dave's whiskers are twitching, it means he's dreaming about something nice.

Messenger Extract

Hill: You left a voicemail saying I should call you

Ed: Big Box, can you call me

Hill: There's no reception here

Ed: Call me from your dad's house phone

Hill: Roger won't let me call a mobile number

Ed: Can you offer to pay him for the cost of the call

Hill: You could always call me

Ed: Um

Hill: Um

Ed: Um

Hill: What did you want to talk about

Ed: General. Want to listen to some ideas?

Hill: Not sure

Ed: I knew you'd say that and that's why I asked you to call

Hill: You could call me, that's definitely possible. I still think Jack Black might turn out okay

Ed: Um

Hill: I'm saying I still think everything might turn out okay

Ed: Um, maybe

Hill: Um

Ed: Um, maybe, but probably doubtful. We should meet in person. I have time off work

Hill: You should quit. Only do things you love

Ed: Brilliant advice

Hill: Um

Ed: Seems ridiculous that we've seen each other once in six months, three times this year, whatever. When you're back, we should meet

Hill: I don't really have any ideas for anything in any genre of any possible creative outlet

Ed: I meant just meet

Hill: I need to go

Ed: Talented white men meeting for a hangout

Hill: Problematic

Ed: Haha

Ed: Hillary Rodham Clinton

Ed: Always wanted to type that, just to see what it felt like

Ed: Haha

Ed: Okay, forget it.

Email draft written whilst listening to Classic FM 1:45-3:45AM

Hi Jack,

I left a message with your assistant eight(?) weeks ago – he said you would give me a call back later that day(?) Sorry to be so pushy but,

Rare and literal second chance

Hill walks up the steep, narrow path that leads into the pub's beer garden. He stops and looks over the edge of the stone wall and down towards a row of recently built houses, their garden floodlights illuminating uniform rectangles of synthetic grass, chimeneas, and low-backed rattan sofas.

Amazing world, Hill thinks.

A woman in her fifties part-opens a bi-folding door. She stands in the opening and lights a cigarette, the garden spotlight illuminating her face, smoothed, taut, and unmoving as she inhales and exhales.

Meditative, Hill thinks.

Film this, Hill thinks.

The woman steps forward and puts the cigarette out on top of the chimenea.

FFS, Hill thinks.

The woman places her hand inside the pocket of her fluffy white dressing gown and pulls out a cigarette packet.

Rare and literal second chance, Hill thinks.

Hill takes the phone out of his pocket and holds it in landscape. The lens momentarily struggles to focus as Hill zooms in on the woman's face as she lights the new cigarette. The yellow focus indicator settles and Hill touches the red circle at the bottom of the screen. Hill zooms closer; the woman's eyes look tired and puffy, squinting and then widening as they look directly into camera.

Hill ducks down, loses his footing, and briefly slides face first down the path. He listens as the woman shouts at him to stand up and show himself over and over in a broad Mancunian accent. He presses his hands into the ground to stand up, pausing and then lying back down as loose pieces of gravel dig painfully into his bloody palms.

Relaxing, Hill thinks.

Lie here forever, Hill thinks.

The woman shouts something about calling the police. Hill lifts his face out of the dirt and begins to crawl up the remainder of path and towards the pub.

Class anthem

Hill looks up at the Warholian James Dean, Brando, and Errol Flynn posters hanging on the toxic yellow wall. A jukebox and Who Wants To Be A Millionaire? quiz machine light up the corner next to the toilets. Hill looks at his palms then shuts them again as Trudy returns from the bar and places two pints of Carling on the table.

This is definitely my new aesthetic, Trudy says, loudly, Carling spilling from her raised pint glass.

Hill and Trudy's pint glasses touch, clinking together as Beautiful Day by U2 fades out on the jukebox.

Class anthem, Trudy says, grinning.

Class anthem, Hill says, grinning.

Like I Can by Sam Smith begins playing. Trudy makes a heart shape with her hands and faces it in Hill's direction.

Inbox me hun, Trudy says.

Check your messages hun, Hill says.

Hill drinks one third of his Carling and places the pint glass down on the table. He part opens his hand palm side up, flinches, then closes it tightly. He looks over towards the door, the Millionaire machine, the Brando. The woman behind the bar picks up a tray of used pint glasses and carries them through a low archway and out of sight.

'Soap's Sexiest Barmaids 2008', Hill thinks.

Trudy looks over towards the bar and back towards Hill. She picks up her Carling and takes a drink, then another.

I want you to start telling me things about you, Trudy says, slurring her words slightly. She picks up her Carling. The glass makes a loud noise as she clumsily places it back down on the table, a steady drip of displaced lager now running over the table's edge and onto the Victorian tiled floor.

Hill looks at the two men sitting at the bar, openly smirking and nudging each other.

Horny bootcut pagans, Hill thinks.

Say or do something, Hill thinks.

Hill opens and shuts his hand three times in succession, for less than a second on each occasion.

Damn, Hill thinks.

Talk to me about something real, tell me the truth about something, Trudy says, agitated and looking back towards the men sitting at the bar.

Lil Naz X is this generation's Frank Sinatra, Hill says, immediately cringing.

Fuck off, Hill, Trudy says.

Her lips pursed and ears bright red, Trudy stares down at the table-top as she picks at the skin around her index finger.

Hill looks at the James Dean on the wall, curling up at the edges inside the cheap plastic frame. Sing by Ed Sheeran begins playing on the jukebox. Hill watches as Trudy acknowledges the song, half-heartedly rolls her eyes, and smiles sadly.

I recognise this is equally funny and insane, Hill says. But when the police told me that Lucy was dead, my first feeling was relief that I wouldn't have to see her family again.

Hill— Trudy says.

When they heard about Jack Black their first response was to say how awful Gulliver's Travels was, Hill says. I don't know what I did to deserve that. It just seemed pathological. It was difficult for Lucy. I don't ever want to see a single one of them again. I assume Roger told you about the ashes...

Oh, Hill, Trudy says.

Hill's stares at the old gas fire, its heat panels blackened like burnt toast, and then up at the Welsh flag tacked to the wall above. The flag has You Don't Fuck With The Môn stencilled on it in large white block capitals.

Belligerence, Hill thinks.

Roger definitely told you about the ashes, it's fine, Hill says.

Trudy leans over towards Hill and says something he can't make out. Taking his hand and slowly prising it open, she runs her fingers over his. He feels a stinging sensation as her lips press down on the exposed patches of punctured and raw skin dotted over his palm, his mind blanking momentarily.

This island could sink and we could live in a new underwater island city

Hill parks away from the other cars in the car park. He is wearing one of Roger's weatherproof coats. Roger paid one hundred and fifty pounds for it over a decade ago and it has probably been worn less than thirty times.

Does this coat age me somehow, Hill thinks.

Weatherproof, weather resistant, waterproof, water resistant, how many more, Hill thinks.

Trudy is craning her neck around towards the boot and talking to Ralph, her denim skirt riding up to the tops of her thighs. Hill stares for a moment then turns to face the windscreen and watch as a group of adults, children, and dogs get out of an old Renault Espace and walk towards the forest trail that runs parallel to the beach. As the family walks out of sight, Hill listens to Trudy asking Ralph whether he is excited to go for a walk, whether he is excited to go swimming, whether he is excited to possibly see some of his friends walking or swimming too, whether he is excited to wear himself out for the day, whether he is excited to be in Hill's new movie.

Please, you said you wouldn't put any pressure on this, Hill says.

Hill's being a negatoid, Ralphy, Trudy says.

Hill looks at his palms. He recalls the week before his mother died, the two of them sitting in the bath, comparing the wrinkles on their fingers, Hill struggling to keep up as she spoke about her hopes for him, the house, Roger, and her future in increasingly antagonistic and abstract terms.

Hill becomes conscious that Trudy is looking in his direction and turns to face her.

I want to do this, Hill says. It doesn't matter what it is, but I want to feel like making something is still possible, or conceivable or whatever.

Trudy leans back on the seat, closes her eyes and smiles.

Hill looks at his palms, Trudy, his phone screen, Trudy, the reedy sand dunes that form a barrier between the car park and the beach. He remembers the day of his mother's funeral and Roger's ashen, miserable face; the mourners from his mother's book club, all stoned, not knowing how to explain suicide to an eleven-year-old; how empty the house felt to him, the silence inside his bedroom as he stood in front of the floor-length mirror and stared at himself for as long as he could take before blinking and starting again.

Hill takes his phone, holds it in front of his face, and begins recording.

***

The beach runs for approximately two miles in either direction. The entrance to the beach has been made from bulldozed sand dunes. To the left of the entrance is the 'dogs permitted' side.

You can take a golden retriever or spaniel and walk along the beach and then around towards the marshland. Once at the marshland you can walk up the sand dunes and stand and look across the strait towards the mainland. Mostly all you can see here are a couple of large houses, partially obscured by dense expanses of trees. Often there will be yachts or motorboats in the water, making their way to or from Caernarfon.

To the right of the entrance is the 'dogs not permitted' side. You can walk along the beach and not have to worry about golden retrievers or spaniels. If you keep walking you can join a path that will take you up to a disused lighthouse that was used as a location in a Demi Moore and Sean Bean movie. You can walk either to the left or to the right, both are valid options depending on what you want to do and what your expectations are.

***

Hill, Trudy, and Ralph return to the car three hours later. Ralph has exhausted himself and Trudy has to lift him into the car boot. She is covered in sand and brushes herself down.

It's getting dark, we should leave, Hill says.

They get in the car. Hill feels tired and hungry.

Grossman pasta, Hill thinks.

I want to look at the footage, Trudy says. She leans over towards Hill and rests her head on his shoulder and closes her eyes.

I wouldn't normally, I mean— Hill says.

I really just want to look at what we filmed, that's all I want to do, Trudy says.

Hill feels her breath on his neck and then takes the iPhone out of his pocket and opens the video album. He presses play and they watch a thirty-second clip of Ralph barking at the top of a sand dune.

He's such a handsome jerk, so self-aware, Trudy says.

Hill presses play and they watch a ten-second clip of a gull in the sky.

So aimless, Trudy says. *Gullcore*, I love it.

Hill presses play and they watch a fifty-five-second clip of Hill running up a large sand dune.

Hunk, Trudy says.

Hill presses play and they watch a seventy-second clip of Trudy running up a large sand dune.

Baddest bitch, Trudy says.

Hill presses play and they watch a ninety-second clip of Hill standing at the edge of the sea.

You look happy there, Trudy says.

Hill presses play and they watch a twenty-second close-up of Trudy laughing.

I just snorted on my feature film debut, Trudy says.

Hill presses play and they watch a five-second clip of Trudy placing her hand on Hill's face and saying something that the iPhone microphone doesn't pick up.

Hill presses play and they watch one-second of a ten-second clip of Lucy, tanned and smiling, standing bolt upright in front of an Orla Kiely feature wall.

I think we got some good footage, Hill says. Some of it's, um, maybe. I don't know. Thank you for helping me.

We could go and get some food and then maybe go to my friend's house party? Trudy says, smiling, looking straight ahead.

That seems, um, okay, Hill says, turning the key to the ignition, looking over to Trudy as she runs her hands through her hair, shaking out the sand.

Co-op car park (~5% capacity)

Hill turns off the engine and looks straight ahead. The car park is at ~5% capacity.

I will never leave here, Hill thinks.

Hill picks up a small box of low calorie toffees and puts two in his mouth.

Don't crunch them, Hill thinks.

Hill crunches the toffees and swallows the pieces as quickly as he can.

Eat when you feel sad, Hill thinks.

He looks across to the empty passenger seat; Trudy is back at her apartment reading journals in preparation for a seminar, meaning no food together but the house party still a grim inevitability.

Hill looks straight ahead at the stone wall that separates the car park from the railway track. The line runs right the way through the island, but this is the only place it stops, and then only on request. Five years ago, Hill stood on the platform waiting for a train with a large group of men, most of whom he barely knew, for a stag weekend in Dublin. Hill didn't know what to say when he was in their company; they had little in common and seemed to view his comments and opinions with suspicion.

I remember all of their names, Hill thinks.

Have they ever Googled me, Hill thinks.

Would they remember my name, Hill thinks.

Hill looks straight ahead at the stone wall. He has driven to the Co-op so he can buy cans for the house party.

Show up with every kind of Pringles instead of alcohol, Hill thinks.

Would Trudy laugh, Hill thinks.

Hill looks straight ahead at the stone wall and listens for the next train to pass through.

Legit house party (pt1/3)

There is no room to park outside the house, so Hill drives slowly past the shabby Georgian terrace and down the steep incline towards the bottom of the road. He pulls up behind an empty skip and watches as a tall, dark-haired man roughly his age walks up the hill, a skateboard in one hand and a visibly straining plastic Morrison's bag in the other.

Don't take drugs or drink too much, Hill thinks.

Don't do anything, at all, Hill thinks.

Hill turns up the volume on the car stereo, rests his head on the car seat and closes his eyes. He is breathing heavily and trying to ignore the phone vibrating inside his trouser pocket.

Please stop, Hill thinks.

The vibrations stop.

Okay, great, Hill thinks.

A sudden banging noise on the driver's side window startles Hill. He jumps in his seat then turns his head. Trudy's face and hands are pressed on the window.

Is her tongue touching the glass, Hill thinks.

Let's go, Trudy says.

Hill watches as Trudy steps away from the car and begins walking up the road. She is wearing an oversized navy blue cable-knit sweater, black leggings, and Berghaus walking boots. She turns back towards the car and pulls a can of Tesco generic lager out of a Morrison's carrier bag. She opens the can and mouths *come on*. Hill's hands grip the steering wheel. He looks at the key, still in the ignition. He looks at the analogue dashboard clock, still broken. He looks at his hands, still tight to the brown plastic wheel surround.

Hill, Trudy shouts.

***

Hi everyone, this is Hill. He's a really talented filmmaker here to try and cast his new movie, Trudy says.

There is muted laughter and a vague feeling of ambivalence. The people at the house party look to be mostly Trudy's age, some older by a few years, probably Hill's age, and some older than that. A great many of the people are wearing cable-knit sweaters and the air is thick with weed smell. Some people pause momentarily, nod and say hi. Trudy looks at Hill and smiles.

Thank you for such a clear introduction, Hill says.

Trudy hugs Hill and says something in his ear that he can't make out. He twice asks her to repeat herself but gives up on the third attempt.

Someone passes Hill a joint and, despite saying no, he takes it and has some. That's nice, he says.

Hill turns to hand Trudy the joint but she's walking down the corridor towards the kitchen. He looks down at the carmine floorboards, badly scuffed and caked with dirt, the weed smoke rising up into his face.

Okay, Hill thinks.

***

A woman with long brown hair, white Asics T-shirt, and green jeans sits down next to Hill. She opens a can of Kronenbourg and passes it to Hill before opening up another can and taking a small sip.

I'm an actor and you're a filmmaker, apparently, she says.

Hill takes a long drink of the Kronenbourg and opens his mouth to speak.

You went to school with my cousin, she says. There's that. What else is there? Do you know Doom? He's here tonight. He's very wild.

'Doom', Hill thinks.

He also went to school with my cousin, so, She continues. Doom's incredibly intelligent. He's forty, but you'd never know it. Doom? Does the name ring a bell, Hill? Doom?

No, it does not, Hill says. I don't think–

Are you sure, because–

Sorry, I just don't think I know anyone called Doom–

Doom said you were like this, She says. What's that face? No, it's chill, Hill. You're a creative. Me too. I'm developing a new modality. There's that. Rad thoughts welcome.

Hill tries to gauge whether she is making fun of him and, regardless, feels hurt and defensive. He thinks about how healthy Jack Black looked, how melancholic he seemed throughout their Skype meeting, how healthy Jack Black's production assistant looked, how scared Jack Black's production assistant looked. He thinks about Trudy and Roger and whether they have spoken together and discussed his life, his mother, Lucy. He thinks about how much he would like to sit down with a four pack and look through the photos on Lucy's Facebook. He remembers that he deleted Lucy's Facebook the day after she died, reactivating it three months later and writing a two-thousand-word status about how their relationship was coming to an end and then she died. He remembers thinking about how their relationship wasn't coming to an end at all. He remembers thinking about how their relationship went through three or four definitive phases over the course of their eight years together. He remembers a conversation about having children that was left open. He remembers a conversation about having children that ended with a clear resolution. He remembers the external hard drive he posted to Roger that has all of the emails, Facebook chat logs, WhatsApp chat logs, Gmail chat logs between him and Lucy. He remembers the Post-it note he stuck on top of the hard drive: *Roger, do not look at this okay. From, Hill.* He remembers other things.

The woman, her pupils dilated, stops talking, seemingly mid-sentence, and presses her fingers down on the dark circles underneath her eyes. Genetic, the bags are genetic, she says.

Hill stares at her, unsure how to respond.

Email drafts written whilst sitting on a toilet 12:00AM

Dear Jack,

Your episode of Seinfeld SOMETHING SOMETHING SOMETHING, SOMETHING ABOUT BEE MOVIE, SOMETHING ABOUT SOMETHING ELSE

SOMETHING ABOUT ME, SOMETHING SOMETHING

SOMETHING SOMETHING SOMETHING ELSE

GOODBYE JACK

Email drafts written whilst sitting on a toilet
12:15AM

Jack,

I am in possession of my wife's ashes. Should I microdose on them every day for a year to prove my love?

What's the worst thing that's ever happened to you (non-career related)? I'm at a house party, for what it's worth

Legit house party (pt2/3)

Hill sits down on a sofa in the living room. The actor has gone but he can still hear her voice somewhere in the background.

Will she 'make it', Hill thinks.

Will she create the one true modality, Hill thinks.

Message Ed about her, Hill thinks.

A man with shoulder-length, receding blond hair and a black cable-knit sweater passes Hill a Kronenbourg and sits down next to him.

Doom told me to find you and talk to you about television, the blond man says, grinning. He said you might have some interesting points of view.

Is Doom here? Hill says.

The blond man looks around the room and shakes his head.

I mean, is he here, in this house?

Doom's pretty much always here, the man replies. Or not.

Taking some coins, bits of paper and tobacco out of his pocket and placing them on the table in front of him, the man runs his hands through his hair and looks up at Hill.

Doom's incredibly–

His real name is Christopher, Hill says.

Incredibly intel–

I'm not trying to be difficult, just–

No, it's all good bro, Doom is Doom, the man replies, taking a
bag of MDMA out of his pocket, opening and tipping its
contents on the battered Ercol table.

Email drafts written whilst sitting on a toilet
1:05AM

Legit house party (pt3/3)

Hill walks out of the upstairs bathroom and looks down the stairs. A couple are standing by the front door, talking to a local homeless man who is standing on the front step. Rogan is well known in the area and Hill remembers watching a documentary about him some years ago. In the documentary, Rogan was filmed smoking heroin in an abandoned boathouse, filmed smoking heroin in a bedsit, filmed smoking heroin outside a post office, filmed smoking heroin in a pub car park, and filmed in a local café, appearing earnestly incredulous at being asked to pay for a fried breakfast.

Hill watches as one of the group, a man with long black hair and a thick beard, reaches down and picks up three bottles of Doom Bar, passing one to Rogan and one to a woman with a skinhead. Rogan looks up, sees Hill looking at them and makes a cheers motion with his bottle. The other two turn towards Hill and laugh before returning to their conversation.

Fucking Rogan, Hill thinks.

Hill turns and looks down the upstairs corridor towards a bedroom. Trudy, sitting on a beanbag, has a MacBook on her lap, the screen light glowing, reflecting onto her face. She turns and looks at Hill.

Hey, hihihihi, Trudy says.

Hill walks into the bedroom and sits on the edge of the futon.

He looks around the room and sees a pile of books, a small desk, a rail with some clothes on, and an empty wicker bin.

I think I feel empathy for whoever lives in this room, Hill says.

Are you enjoying yourself? I'm going to put some music on, Trudy says.

This is great, all of it, Hill says, his head in his hands.

Truly legit house party, Trudy says.

It's incredible, Hill says. Everyone seems so aggressive and forthright with their opinions. Also so serious and defensive. I know that's probably exactly how I'm being perceived, but I don't think they realise how they're behaving. It's fine. I'm having a good time.

Have some of this, it's really weak, Trudy says, passing Hill a small, half-smoked joint. Do you want to look at something on YouTube?

Not as much as I used to, Hill says.

Trudy gets up from the beanbag and sits next to Hill on the futon. She plays a video clip of a Welsh language children's drama from the late nineties.

This looks so cheap and fun, I like it, Hill says. The aesthetic.

No, no, no, look at her, Trudy says. The denim jacket with the mousey hair. Ha. Look at her.

Oh, is that you? Hill says. Oh my God. You look great. I mean, you look so dumb. But you look good on camera. I feel surprised that you haven't told me about this before. You used to be successful.

Thanks, I paid my parents' mortgage off over the five years I was on that programme, Trudy says. I got to keep the clothes. Well, I used to steal the clothes. Everyone at school hated me for a while; I got punched in the mouth once and chipped two of my teeth. I made a lot of money in exchange for being punched, basically.

Trudy takes a long drag from the joint and passes it over to Hill.

But you were successful, Hill says. I'm really turned on by how successful you used to be.

You're so charming, Trudy says. I think acting is okay, problematic in so many ways but whatever. I think it's okay to be on TV, but I was just reading lines, had solid timing, bleep-bleep bloop-bloop blah-blah.

Right, Hill says.

Hill watches Trudy pause the clip on an image of her and two other girls playing pool with colourful plastic tennis rackets.

Too funny, Trudy says.

Trudy stares at the screen for a moment then slowly closes the laptop.

Hill, Trudy says. In a couple of months I'm going to Australia for a year, maybe longer, for the PhD. I'm saying this to you, I'm saying this because of ... I suppose what's going on here.

Well, that's fine, Roger will just have to die alone, Hill says.

I want you to be okay with me going, Hill, Trudy says. Hill?

Sure, Hill says.

You'll be with him, he'll want you there, you're his family, Trudy says. I was reading about the Norwegian whaling season, a whale called Heiko followed a shoal of fish under a narrow bridge that the whaling ship couldn't fit through. The people of Lofoten took her to their hearts; the first time most of them would have seen a living whale. I don't know, humans are generally an abomination, but there's always hope. I really believe that, Hill.

Hill stares at a small area of peeling wallpaper directly above the clothes rail. There isn't a radiator in the room, only single glazed windows, a small single bed, peeling wallpaper, and a clothes rail with ~six items on it.

Why did you let me film you at the beach and not tell me you were a professional actor? Hill says. That's incredibly fucking manipulative.

What? Trudy says. Are you being serious?

I complimented you in good faith.

You 'complimented me in good faith'? Hill, that's ridiculous.

Hill repeatedly attempts to speak but can't get any words out, his eyes drawn to the small 'Doom' scrawled in biro beneath the window ledge. He looks at Trudy and shakes his head. After a moment's pause he leans over and buries his head into her lap, closes his eyes, and listens to her stomach rumbling, drowning out the sound from the party downstairs.

Email from four months ago

Hill, I'm online again. The internet is working, can you believe it!!!111 I'm on a new regime(?) that costs ten pounds a month and everything is so fast. I watched a documentary about Death Row and thought it was an untapped area of potential (speaking comedically). Have you ever thought about this? Have you heard from the production company? Say hello to Ed for me.

I spoke with Patricia and she said that you haven't returned any of their calls recently. Can you please phone them? You really should tell them where you scattered the ashes (I can't quite understand why you are so reluctant?) (It's demented, something your mother might have done, but I digress – and no need to sulk – IT'S JUST AN OBSERVATION).

I'm going for more tests soon. I think it might be an idea, and I think it might be nice, if you were to come and stay for a little while. I'm having a bit of trouble with day to day activities and the alternative is I look for someone to help out. The specialist gave me the name of a support provider (!?) but I'm not sure about that.

I sent you a Skype request, I don't know if you have or haven't seen it? I'll send another, just to be safe.

Potential new mantra (you'd do well to take this on board): Request, Invest, Impress™

Dad

Boutique Village Holds First Annual Seafood Festival

Hill rests his iPhone on Trudy's shoulder, touches the screen and begins recording. Trudy faces the GoPro towards an image of Barack Obama holding a small piece of dark chocolate to his mouth. Obama is in profile, relaxed and unburdened, eating artisanal chocolate made with the island's sea salt. Natasha, Malia, and Michelle Obama are standing in the background, holding hands and smiling calmly. Trudy steps forward and extends her arm so that the GoPro lens is almost touching Obama's mouth.

There is some jostling amongst the small crowd gathered around the Strait Salt stand as the company's founders walk on to elevated platform and hold microphones up to their mouths. They introduce themselves as Laura and Peter. Laura is tall and has long white hair tied in a bun. Peter is tall and wears a fawn checked shirt tucked into baggy red corduroys. Laura and Peter begin talking about their passions and eccentricities, how these traits have kept their marriage as fresh as their business model. The crowd gasps as Peter picks up a piece of sea salt the size of an apple, holds it to his mouth and takes a large bite.

What you see before you is the purest reflection of our commitment to provenance, Laura says, nodding in encouragement as the crowd claps.

Provenance, curiosity, and fun! Peter shouts, wet fragments of sea-salt apple projecting onto the faces at the front of the crowd.

Never give up, laugh all day every day, experiment, your idea is only as real as your rigour, he says, washing down the remaining shards of sea salt with a shot glass of Due Vittorie balsamic vinegar.

Aged twelve years and well worth the wait, Peter says.

'Boutique Village Holds First Annual Seafood Festival', Hill thinks.

Hill turns the iPhone and points it towards Trudy, unsteadily zooming in on her face, the focus drawn gradually towards a scar from her childhood, a thin white line running horizontally through her eyebrow.

Incredible and beautiful, Hill thinks.

Trudy keeps the GoPro pointing towards the stage as Peter speaks, Laura standing to the side and rotating through a series of assured facial expressions and hand gestures. Trudy turns her head slightly and rests her bodyweight on Hill's chest.

Peter stops talking and walks across the stage to embrace Laura. As he takes her hand and raises it above her head, the audience erupts into cheers. Laura and Peter's adult children walk amongst the crowd with trays of sea-salt brioche tasters and prosecco served in branded plastic flutes.

It doesn't get much better than this, guys, Peter says. Welcome all to the salted isle!

It doesn't get much better than this, guys, Trudy says, snorting.

Hill looks towards Peter, now squatting down to talk to an audience member whilst simultaneously using a toothpick to dislodge small salt crystals from in between his teeth.

'Successful Roger', Hill thinks.

Successful Roger didn't kill my mother, Hill thinks.

Actual Roger didn't kill my mother, Hill thinks.

A quiet island

Hill is lying in bed, awake, his eyes open. The room is pitch black, silent. Hill feels cold and pulls the extra blankets up from the bottom of the bed until they cover his neck and the lower half of his face. He can hear himself breathing. The floorboards on the landing creak intermittently. Hill pulls the blankets down a little so that they're not itchy on his face. He looks at the digital alarm clock on the shelf above the washbasin and it reads 01:45.

Suitcase, Hill thinks.

Leave until return flight, Hill thinks.

Ashely Graham Instagram Presence, Hill thinks.

Hill sighs and moves his hand down his pyjama bottoms towards his penis.

The bedroom is directly opposite Roger's room, and although his door is tightly shut, Hill can hear Roger coughing, intermittently moaning, mumbling to himself.

Hill sighs and moves his hand out of his pyjama bottoms.

Do not look at your phone, do not pick up your phone, Hill thinks.

Roger starts coughing again, then moaning, this time more intensely and for longer.

Hill? Roger says, straining, sounding in moderate discomfort.

Hill closes his eyes, holds his breath, and repeats A Quiet Island, slowly and deliberately, until he falls asleep.

Kayaking (A Quiet Island)

There is one blue kayak out in front of the five red kayaks. The man in the blue kayak has curly shoulder-length black hair that sticks out of the sides of his small black helmet, a small silver hoop piercing in his right ear, and thick salt and pepper stubble over his face. The man makes his kayak turn around to face the red kayaks. He manoeuvres his paddle, holding his position in the water. He speaks to the teenage boys and girls in the red kayaks and they look at him with determined, happy, worried, happy, bored facial expressions. The teenagers in the red kayaks are finding it difficult to keep their kayaks under control. The man begins shouting a series of instructions, plans for how they will kayak in between the arches of the bridge, the plan being to make a figure of eight motion. This will help them to master the art of steering, the man in the blue kayak is shouting.

The teenagers in the red kayaks follow the man in the blue kayak as he begins the first figure of eight. All of the teenagers manage okay and the man in the blue kayak tells them they're on their own now and need to do six more figures of eight before they can paddle back to the slipway and go on their lunch break. The man in the blue kayak sits in his kayak and looks up to the sky. It's raining very lightly as he opens his mouth and feels the rain on his tongue. He checks that the teenagers are okay. The teenagers are okay. He pulls the arm of his waterproof jacket up a little and looks at his watch. He looks at the stonework of the bridge from as high as he can make out back down to sea level; a seagull is standing on some yellow foam membrane that has washed onto the wider, semi-submerged stone blocks that take the bridge's supporting pillars down to the seabed. The man in the blue kayak watches as the seagull propels itself off the seaweed and into the sky. He checks that the teenagers are okay. The teenagers are okay. He pulls the arm of his waterproof jacket up a little and looks at his watch. The man in the blue kayak shouts, Good enough let's go, let's go.

Dolphin sighting (A Quiet Island)

A medium-sized motorboat picks up a group of eight people from the pier. The people are happy. They are happy because they are going to see dolphins swimming in the wild. There is a strong chance they will see a pod swimming together, and in exceptional circumstances they may see a superpod containing hundreds of dolphins. People love dolphins, the more of them the better. Human knowledge of dolphins is increasing exponentially. Dolphins are intelligent beings, this has always been recognised, but people now know that they talk to each other and greet one another with personalised and specific clicks. Names, in other words. Dolphins have names for each other. People feel happy when they see dolphins.

As the boat passes underneath the larger of the two bridges that connect the island to the mainland, a small boy leans over the edge of the boat and throws up. He throws up continuously until the first sighting of dolphins. The man driving the boat shouts and points ahead and to the right. The small boy wipes the sick and saliva off his mouth and onto the padded inside of the boat. He begins smiling, then pointing, then nudging his mother, then laughing. People feel happy when they see dolphins.

On the way back to the pier the water is choppy and people talk less, holding on to the rails tighter and tighter, looking straight ahead with serious or worried facial expressions. The man driving the boat shouts, Just a moment everyone, not a problem. He is unsure whether any of the passengers can hear him and repeats himself.

The water is less choppy once the boat re-enters the strait, but it's started raining now and the people on the boat are getting wet. The rain starts coming down harder, driving into people's faces. The rain turns into hail, then back into rain again. Some people are laughing, but a Mancunian woman in her fifties says, *Get me off this bloody boat*. The dolphins are probably carrying on with what they were doing before they saw the humans. They are capable of fun, they play complex games amongst themselves with rules and outcomes. Dolphins are also capable of seemingly arbitrary violence against one another too, a terrifying thought, but one that only makes them more comparable to humans.

The small boy turns his head and looks back in the direction of the dolphin sighting, beyond the smaller suspension bridge, beyond the larger bridge, beyond the point where the strait meets the Irish sea. He pulls out his phone and looks at the photos he took of the dolphins. They are bad photos, mostly blurred, but he finds one good one and makes it his new lock-screen photo.

The people on the boat arrive back at the pier, get off the boat and either go to the pub or back to their holiday cottages.

Great mates, inseparable, football, table tennis

Hill looks at the list of items on Roger's most recent weekly shopping list, mundane items mixed in with his latest whims and obsessions. Hill sighs as he pushes the trolley towards the fruit and vegetable aisle and chooses four loose carrots, four loose red onions, and two large potatoes. Hill looks again at the list and sees that Roger has written something indecipherable next to 'porridge'. Hill crumples the list, puts it back in his trouser pocket, and pushes the trolley towards the alcohol aisle.

Aimlessly staring at the craft beer section, Hill hears a distantly familiar voice. Listening for a moment Hill realises it is Stuart Penry, loosely speaking a friend from school. Hill and Stuart's friendship arc could be assessed as:

Year Seven: Great mates, inseparable, football, table tennis.

Year Eight: Great mates, inseparable, football, table tennis.

Year Nine: Great mates, Hill listened to Ready To Die on repeat, Stuart listened to Ocean Drive on repeat.

Year Ten: Mates, Hill experimented with right-wing politics, Stuart experimented with girls and listened to Ocean Drive on repeat.

Year Eleven: Mates/Non-Mates, Hill looked at the internet, Stuart had sex with girls and listened to Ocean Drive on repeat.

Year Twelve: Non-Mates, Hill read Empire, Stuart fell in love with the head girl and listened to Ocean Drive on repeat.

Year Thirteen: Non-Mates, Hill read Sight & Sound, Stuart fell in love with the new head girl and listened to Ocean Drive on repeat.

Continue looking at beer, Hill thinks.

Shitty names for these beers, Hill thinks.

Looking straight ahead, Hill picks up and scans the labels of every single bottle of beer in the craft section. He can still hear Stuart's voice, a peculiarly generic placeless drone, like a voiceover from a toothpaste advert.

He's seen me and is waiting for me to do something, Hill thinks.

Take control, Hill thinks.

Hill turns to speak to Stuart but sees that Stuart's back is to him and he is talking on a mobile. Stuart still seems in good shape physically, apart from a prominent bald patch around the crown of his head. Hill smiles and feels good about himself and his full head of hair. He thinks it strange that Stuart hasn't shaved his head, that he is happy to have such a glaringly obvious bald patch. He thinks it strange that Stuart has never been on any social media and revisits a long-held theory that Stuart took that stance to avoid the awkwardness that would arise when it came to their relationship.

Am I a delusional human being, Hill thinks.

Hill considers how he could just leave, how Stuart would never know he had been there, how he could walk away victorious and tell Roger that his old friend Stuart was a balding loser with shitty prospects and no online presence.

Full head of hair delusion syndrome, Hill thinks.

Pick up some beer and walk away, Hill thinks.

Hill picks up the beer and looks at the illustration on the bottle of a steampunk surf-pirate. Hill would only buy craft beer with other people's money, in this instance Roger's. The inheritance he received from his mother was still enough to last him a couple of years if he was careful. He had enough for rent on the studio, utilities, food, generic brand supermarket lager. At first, he enjoyed living like this. In the aftermath of Lucy dying, he found the inflexible routine of having a small, fixed budget a great comfort. Time spent looking for cheap products, walking from supermarket to supermarket; the hours spent slowly drinking Tesco French lager whilst staring at the studio walls all seemed like a consistent, balanced existence.

Nothing bad happens when nothing happens, Hill thinks.

Pick up the beer and leave, Hill thinks.

Hill crouches down to pick up a reduced four pack of Tiny Rebel and feels a hand on his shoulder. He twists his head to look up and sees Stuart's face looking back at him. Hill feels his heart rate increase exponentially, instinctively pressing his hand against his chest.

Oh God, Hill thinks.

Bloody cheapskate, Stuart says, motioning at the bottles of Tiny Rebel.

Hi Stu—, Hill says.

Are you shorter than you used to be? You look small, Stuart says.

I think I'm probably the same height, Hill says.

Hill looks at Stuart's shopping basket; a copy of Top Marques magazine and a large discounted pork pie, both partially obscured by several pouches of Strait Salt.

For a casual supper we're hosting tomorrow, Stuart says. Best accompanied with a few cheeky shots of Due Vittorie I find.

Did you go to the seafood festival last week? Hill says.

After a long pause, Stuart looks at his watch and says he has to get home to his wife and kids. He takes his phone out of his trouser pocket and suggests he and Hill swap numbers.

Great, Hill says.

Why, Hill thinks.

Hill stands and watches as Stuart uses Siri to register Hill as a new contact.

Hill from school, Stuart says.

Hill from school, Stuart says.

Hill from school, Stuart says.

'Hill from school', Hill thinks.

Music to win to

Hill and Trudy arrive at the leisure centre. Hill parks away from the other cars and turns the engine off. He is wearing an unbranded loose-fit black T-shirt, pale blue shorts, and a pair of brown Asda trainers. Trudy is wearing a Nike headband, navy cable-knit sweater, green and white Dunlop shorts, red Converse.

Are we going in with a strategy, playing to win, steamrolling these mothers? Trudy says.

I think we need to go, play for half an hour, make an excuse about Roger and then leave, Hill says.

Feel like we should be listening to DMX or some such, Trudy says. Music to win to.

What, um, I don't know, Hill says.

Hill is sweating a little. He doesn't want to see Stuart again. He has been dreaming about school every night for the last week, wondering how much of his career the people in his year have followed, specifically how much research Stuart has done. He tries to imagine what Stuart would think of the Jack Black situation. He tries to imagine what kind of film Stuart would pay to see at the cinema. He tries to imagine what kind of film Stuart and his wife watch at home once their children have gone to bed. He tries to imagine what Stuart's wife looks like, whether she's better or worse looking than head girl number one, head girl number two, Lucy, Trudy.

But we're playing to win? Trudy says, reaching across to Hill and putting her hand on his leg and squeezing it, smiling.

We're definitely playing to win, Hill says.

***

Hill and Stuart walk over to a table. Stuart is wearing a full Arsenal kit with the socks pulled up and folded over just below the knees. His shoes are expensive looking training shoes, neon orange with a bright blue mesh covering the toes.

Casual knock-up? Stuart says.

Hill throws the table tennis ball in the air, lets it bounce and plays a shot straight into the net.

Fuck, man, Hill says.

You shut your eyes, Stuart says. Pro tip: don't do that.

Stuart throws a ball in the air and plays a slow, high, and central serve across to Hill.

Don't patronise me, Hill says, playing a deliberately slow and looping backhand across to Stuart.

We're just lads having a casual knock-up, Stuart says, playing a forehand return that drives towards the back of the table.

Hill becomes more confident in his play and starts hitting the ball harder and with topspin. He moves Stuart around the table and begins winning the rallies.

Die, Hill thinks.

Would you go to a reunion? Hill says.

Yeah, of course... I mean, we did, three years ago, Stuart says, playing an aggressive forehand.

We? Hill thinks.

The ball bounces up and hits Hill on the nose before he can readjust his position. Hill picks the ball up from the floor and makes a show of inspecting it for cracks.

What did people say about me, Hill thinks.

Better to be an enigma, Hill thinks.

I wasn't there, Hill says. He picks up the ball and serves it over to Stuart.

Yeah, pretty lame, Stuart says. I see most of them anyway, but some of the randoms were just absolutely classic.

Hill returns the ball, attempting a backhand spin that does nothing. Stuart plays a mis-hit backhand straight into the air. He reaches his bat up and hits the ball over to Hill's side of the table.

Clemmy Edwards is still a total slag by the way, Stuart laughs. That's all I can say in this environment, but details available on request from Pete Bane.

Hill waits for the ball's bounce to reach the highest point and angrily attempts an overhead smash that goes way too high and deep, missing the table by two or three metres.

Clemmy who? Hill says.

***

Trudy plays an overhead smash and beats Stuart's wife 21-0.

Trudy plays an overhead smash and beats Stuart's wife 21-0.

Trudy plays an overhead smash and beats Stuart's wife 21-0.

All-court Serena game, Hill thinks.

Hill, Trudy, Stuart, Stuart's wife walk out of the table tennis hall, Stuart turning into the men's changing area as the rest continue onwards in silence.

Hill, Trudy, and Stuart's wife queue up at the cafeteria till with their drinks.

Hill, Trudy, and Stuart's wife sit down on fixed plastic chairs and sip from their sports drinks. Stuart, now in a change of clothes, sits down with them.

So I heard you were making a film and that? Stuart says.

Hill nods his head. Trudy puts the bottle of energy drink to her mouth and drinks half.

So is it on Netflix or? Stuart says, opening and then closing Netflix on his phone.

Trudy puts the bottle of energy drink to her mouth and takes a long sip.

You want a major studio involved, Stuart says. If this is your one decent idea, it has to get out there.

Hill, slumped in his chair, his arms tightly folded in on themselves, looks at Trudy as she fixes a stare on Stuart.

Stuart, what do you do? Trudy says.

Well, this has been really great, Hill says. But, my dad is ill and...

I know, hope he gets better soon, Stuart says. The legend.

What? Hill says. How do you know about Roger?

So I helped him out with some stocks last year, sent a few choice cuts for his portfolio, Stuart says. Can't win them all though, but that's the market. Roger gets it. Do you still fish?

I have never fished, Hill says. I don't. Wait, what market?

So we were fishing and these dolphins, Stuart says, laughing loudly. These ridiculous dolphins are swimming close to our boat and–

No, Hill thinks.

Hill looks at Trudy, her left hand gripping the energy drink, her shoulder stiff.

So Laura actually catches one, a baby, Stuart says, laughing, the upper half of his body shaking. It's... she...she actually has it hanging there off a line, a baby fucking dolphin. I was pissing myself.

Hill looks at Trudy, a wild look in her eyes.

Hill looks at Laura, Stuart's wife, laughing along but urging restraint, her hand on Stuart's leg, squeezing.

So the dolphin is making these noises, thrashing everywhere, Stuart says. Just incredibly—

Was the dolphin experiencing pain and fear, do you think? Trudy says, grinning, her eyes locked on Stuart.

Just, it was just, so funny, Stuart laughs.

Stuart, it's a question, Trudy says. I'm asking you a question.

Fine, yes, probably, Stuart says. It was just, just incredibly, incredibly funny.

It actually, it's bad, but, actually, God, it was, it really, really was *eff-ing funny*, Laura says, a tear rolling down her cheek.

Stuart, laughing uncontrollably, Laura, simultaneously laughing and grimacing, both reliving the moment so lucidly, appear to temporarily depart the astral plane.

Don't look at Trudy, Hill thinks.

Hill looks at Trudy, jaw clenched and eyes frozen, unblinking.

So we're going to make a move, mate, Stuart says, wiping a tear from his eye. Kids are with their grandparents today and that?

Okay, Hill says.

I'll call you and we can have some beers yeah, really catch up, Stuart says. I'll get Bane, Pinney, and Adams involved. It'll be a smash.

Sure, Hill says.

Absolutely not, Hill thinks.

Stuart smiles and moves in to embrace Hill, wrapping his arms around Hill's back and squeezing, briefly attempting to lift him, saying something that Hill can't make out.

Smells the same as fifteen years ago, Hill thinks.

Lynx Africa, Hill thinks.

Over Stuart's shoulder Hill looks across the cafeteria to Trudy; her nose is pressed against the glass wall that looks down onto the swimming pool. She has a neutral facial expression, her eyes focused on a small boy hesitating on the top diving board. She mouths something as the boy eventually jumps, her eyes following him down to the water and watching as his head bobs back up again moments later. Hill pulls away from Stuart and waves him and his wife off as they walk towards the stairs, watching as Stuart's wife puts her hand in the back pocket of his baggy fawn chinos.

Hill looks at them. They are happier than he is, and they know it.

Basic pagan couple, Hill thinks.

Hill hears Trudy calling him over to the glass window. He smiles and thinks about lying down with Trudy in a room full of sleeping Boxers, closing his eyes and drifting off to the sound of their collective snores.

Norwegian fuckers

Do you want to drive, or should I drive? Trudy says. She is pushing Ralph back into the house, his tail wagging, relentlessly banging against the wooden door frame, long tongue flopping around his mouth, dark eyes full of optimism. Ralph's basket is always in the kitchen now. Each morning when Hill wakes up and comes down for a smoothie he looks at the brown plastic oval next to the radiator, the kitchen smelling more and more of Ralph every day. Trudy has been staying at the house two or three nights a week, getting up in the middle of the night to sit with Roger through his coughing fits; Hill lying awake in his bed, cold, trying not to retch at the sound of an apparently endlessly regenerating supply of phlegm.

Ralph moves into the house and Trudy shuts the back door. Do you think I need to lock this? she says.

Yes, I do think you need to lock the back door, Hill says. He is wearing a pair of walking boots recently bought from TK Maxx, thirty pounds down from a hundred and twenty, skinny black trousers, and a aubergine raincoat. I think we need to leave, we need to leave right now to get there in time for the film, he says.

Are we late? I think there's enough time, Trudy says. Do you want to drive? Or do you want me to drive?

I'd probably never choose to drive anywhere, Hill says. Thank you for offering.

Trudy looks over to Hill. He is reading the back of a CD case, a 90s dance anthems compilation. You're being very quiet, Hill, she says. Quiet Hill is here, should we fear him?

I'm reading this, but I'm thinking about the film as well, Hill says. I've been looking forward to it, and I didn't think they'd show it anywhere round here. I usually go to the cinema alone, by the way.

No, that's fine, Trudy says. I'm a great cinema date. I'm excited to eat at Pizza Hut. It's like we're teenagers and I'm the older one who passed their test first.

Trudy jabs Hill on the arm, the punch hitting harder than she intended.

Sorry, I have brothers, Trudy says. I told them about you, by the way.

Hill looks out of the window and down towards the strait as a large commercial fishing boat moves slowly towards the Irish sea.

I'm a competent driver, Hill says, I just don't enjoy it. I'll drive on the way back if you want. I passed on my first attempt. What about you, when did you pass your test?

What do you mean?

I mean, when did you pass your test?

No, I didn't really do that.

What?

I just never got around to it, or lessons, I just learnt watching my dad, my brothers, some boyfriends, Trudy says. I'm pretty comfortable behind the wheel. Lol at 'behind the wheel', that sounds funny to me, like something Roger might say.

Hill puts the CD case back in the side compartment and watches closely as Trudy moves the gearstick from third to fourth and then up to fifth.

***

The film is two hours and twenty minutes. It's about young Norwegian people who are calm for most of the time, even when life is very trying in their share-house. Some of the young Norwegians have jobs at places like cafés, libraries, record shops, and small offices. One of the young Norwegians does not work and has set his sights on never working. It is through this person's eyes that the audience sees the majority of the film. He has a girlfriend who is Norwegian but works as a teacher in China. We don't see this character because the broadband in the share-house is broken. Outside of work hours we see the young Norwegians playing board games, drinking beer, and sitting in the bath talking about the people they know.

The young Norwegians are wearing oversized cable-knit sweaters for ninety percent of the film.

Hill looks over towards Trudy; engrossed, she is leaning forward, her chin resting on her hands as her elbows rest on her knees.

Concentrate harder, enjoy this more than her, Hill thinks.

Truly hate this film, Hill thinks.

Trudy turns her head and smiles. She looks emotional. She looks like she is trying to hide how emotional she is. She looks determined to appear happy and serious and engaged. Trudy does a thumbs up gesture and turns back towards the screen, her feet banging against the seat in front of her.

Hill makes a shushing noise and looks straight ahead, clenching and unclenching his jaw muscles repeatedly.

***

The Pizza Hut is mostly empty, there are customers on a table near the front window, tired and bored looking. One of the staff is sitting at a table in the corner looking at his phone and eating mozzarella sticks. His face is tanned and he has an intricate beard made up of a series of overlapping equilateral triangles.

Did you prefer that to White House Down? I really loved it, Trudy says. She is holding a slice of spicy vegan pizza in one hand and gripping a large glass of Sprite in the other. She has eaten over half of her pizza in the time it has taken Hill to finish a single slice.

It was fine, maybe I was underwhelmed or, Hill says. That's probably why I'm eating so slowly. Experiencing disappointment kills my appetite.

You really seemed like you were enjoying it though, Trudy says. I thought it was good, a solid seven point five. Did you find the characters annoying? Halfway through I thought: I bet Hill hates these Norwegian fuckers.

Why would you think I'd hate them, Hill says.

I think I understand what you don't like better than what you do like, Trudy says. If you gave my friends a chance you'd probably like them a little bit more. I mean, it's cool, it really is. I don't mind...

Probably your friends, I don't know, Hill says. I think they took an instant dislike to me maybe. They seem suspicious or unwelcoming to outsiders. I mean, it's fine, it really is.

Hill takes a long drink from his pint glass of Coke. He picks up a slice of pizza and takes a bite. Trudy is staring at him unblinkingly.

Wish I'd never met this person, Hill thinks.

I am alive and having a nice time in Pizza Hut, Hill thinks.

Glad I met this person, Hill thinks.

***

Staring straight ahead at the now empty road, Hill turns the volume down on the radio.

I grew up here, Hill says. I don't know how I would describe that experience. Probably pretty okay for most of the time, it's just when people start to romanticise things it gets, um. It's better to be honest if you can. Also I think it's okay to forget things, like negative experiences that serve no positive purpose in your life. I'd include friends in that.

Hill, Trudy says.

I don't mean your friends, I'm not passing any comment on them. They haven't impacted me at all, either positive or negative. I'm talking about my experience.

Stop being like this, Hill thinks.

Trudy looks tired, and for the first time Hill notices small age lines around her eyes. He looks at her lips, her eyelashes, her eyebrows, and all look exactly how Hill would picture them in his head when she's not around.

Trudy nods her head, one hand on the wheel and the other trying to force a Wrigley's Extra out of a crumpled packet.

Better driver than me, Hill thinks.

Better person overall, Hill thinks.

I was looking at the footage we got, Hill says, I might edit it on Roger's computer. We could do some more filming if it looks okay. I don't know, maybe...

Why do you call your dad Roger? Trudy says.

Hill turns the volume up on the car radio.

Hill–

I call him Roger because he is Roger, Hill says.

Email from twelve months ago

Hello again, Hill. I tried calling you again earlier this week but you didn't answer. Does your answer machine(?) work? I have been sorting through your room and found some marvellously detailed school reports, would you like them?

Sample extract: A solid effort that was unfortunately not matched in terms of attainment.

Sample extract: Hill needs to speak up more during class rather than remain so introverted.

Sample extract: Has shown no aptitude for swimming, although his basketball skills have improved somewhat.

Well, you get the picture! I could spend all day reading them, they do make me laugh. Should I make photostats and post them to you? Or perhaps you can look at them the next time you're here (which will be when exactly?!!111).

How are things coming along with the script? Do say hello to Ed for me (is he still with Laura?)

I spoke with Patricia again, she asked after you. If you ever want to talk about Lucy you should give your cousin Thomas a call, he's been studying counselling at college, an NVQ of some kind (wishy washy nonsense if you ask me!) and could do with the practice I should think.

I'll be going for some tests at the hospital again. Nothing to worry about, I'm certainly not in any case. You mustn't worry about me, concentrate on yourself and improving your own fortunes, Hill. I'll leave you with this: Productivity Births Profit™ (think about it!)

Feel strong aversion to this

Roger told me to tell you that he called Mike McCarthy, your old English teacher, and spoke with him about you going into Rose College and doing a talk for the A Level class? Trudy says. She's grinning and waving a rolled up Financial Times in front of Ralph's face.

Grrrrr, Ralph, Grrrrrrrrrrrr, Trudy says, making the dog bark louder and jump higher.

Hill is wearing a decade old grey Carhartt T-shirt he found in a drawer in his bedroom. There is a tear around the collar and small holes in the armpit areas. Hill stands up and puts his hands on top of his head.

I can't believe he did that, Hill says. No, I can. He knows how much I won't want to do that. What a dick. I am in no way even going to consider it. Does it strike you that every single thing he does is intended to make my life miserable?

He said they'd be willing to pay you, Trudy says. They started charging foreign students double or something. Either way, they have money there.

Feel strong aversion to this, Hill says. I never thought I'd go back there.

Hill sits at the kitchen table and turns the volume down on the radio.

You always have this so loud, Hill says. It actually makes it harder to hear what's being said on there somehow. I feel so much scepticism about going back there. How much did he say they'd pay? It doesn't matter, I'm not doing it.

You said you liked your English teacher?

No.

You did!

No. I—

You did, I remember you said you liked him, Trudy says.

No, I said that I enjoyed going to get DVDs from Blockbuster with him, Hill says. The women who worked there found him attractive, they liked his accent. He told me that one day football wouldn't seem so important. I thought he was crazy. There was this girl in English, he encouraged me to pursue her but it was half-arsed, he didn't give a shit really. Is it difficult to encourage someone and do it properly? No, it's happening already, so much negativity.

Hill grimaces and puts his hands palms down on the table. We've run out of Innocent, again, he says.

Who was the girl from English? Definitely feel like I want to have this insight or something, Trudy says, sitting down opposite Hill.

I don't know, um, Hill says. Clemmy. She came to the school later. There was a rumour she sat on a gearstick in someone's car. She lived here but she was English, or had an English accent. I don't know. She sat next to me and seemed to enjoy my company. In no way did she view me as a sexual being. Please stop laughing. She started going out with someone in the year below. That felt humiliating somehow. I don't think she realised I liked her.

She realised, Trudy says.

Yeah, she did. Clearly. This is so fucked. I feel like crap—

Just find it funny, Trudy says. It's joyous and funny. You have no reason to shy away from the most abysmal failures of your childhood. What does she do now?

She's a teacher in Dubai, I think.

'I think', Trudy says, grinning.

She's a teacher in Dubai, Hill says.

Dubai lifestyle babe, Trudy says.

Okay, shut up, Hill says. It would never have worked between us.

Wouldn't it have worked? Really, would it not? Trudy says.

Yes, I sound like a maniac, Hill says. McCarthy knew she wouldn't be interested, regardless he gave me some vague encouragement to 'go for it'. He probably could have gone a bit more specific. How do I remember all of this, I earnestly do sound insane. Do you want to go out for some food later?

Only if you agree to do the school thing, Trudy says.

Oh God, Hill says. Find out how much they're paying.

Trip Advisor **** restaurant

This restaurant has the best vegan options on the island, Hill, Trudy says. She is holding the menu up in front of her face, slowly fanning herself.

I don't know, Hill says. Most Thai sauces contain fish oil. The waiter seemed spooked when I asked about it. Maybe the one on this menu truly doesn't, that's fine. I have no way of knowing.

I mean, you're not actually vegan though, Trudy says.

Spiritually–

But not *actually*–

But, spiritually, so–

You're like Roger sometimes, Trudy says. It's funny and exhausting. Did Roger obsess over the sugar content of cereals when you were a kid?

No, he didn't. We never ate cerea—

Oh, yeah. Seems like this is his mission now, Trudy says. He printed me a list of cereals that claimed to be healthy but actually contained something crazy like a kilo of sugar per bowl. That's probably not accurate, but, you know.

I'm not like Roger, Hill says.

You are like Roger, Trudy says.

I don't want to talk about Roger—

Okay, we won't talk about Roger tonight, Trudy says.

The waiter's coming over, you order first, I'm still thinking, Hill says. He lifts the menu up in front of his face and lets his eyes lose focus until he can't read the text.

Ready to die a violent death

Hill stops walking and takes the rucksack off his shoulders. He places it at his feet and crouches down to open it. He puts one hand on the floor and feels wet, mushy leaves and pine needles press against his palm. He wipes the hand on his trouser leg and then puts it down to the floor again, this time in a fist. Hill walked through this wood many times as a teenager, but only in the daytime, and even then getting lost sometimes. The trees are tall and densely packed, the path stopping abruptly and splintering into several offshoots that are designed to take visitors on an 'organic trail experience' to various parts of the woods and the beach.

Can't really see anything, Hill thinks.

Hill remembers the beach as being small, the woodland partly wrapping around it to create a muddy, bog-like border composed of pebbles, fallen branches, and sand.

Dark, Hill thinks.

Dark, Hill thinks.

Hill feels around in the rucksack and finds himself constantly touching the same items over and over:

Biro

Apple

Crumpled piece of A4 paper

Crumpled piece of A4 paper

Biro

Hill is looking for his phone. He hasn't turned it on for days but brought it out with him tonight to record Trudy, who promised that there would be different people at the beach party.

Hill finds the phone and takes it out of the bag. He turns on the torch light app and holds the phone up at head height.

This light is worse than no light, Hill thinks.

Is this what death is, Hill thinks.

Suddenly terrified, Hill thinks.

Hill looks at the phone's screen and tries to find a way to make the torch app shine brighter. He notices that the battery indicator is flashing at 1%.

Horror film, Hill thinks.

Will die in this forest, Hill thinks.

Am ready to die a violent death, Hill thinks.

The phone makes the shutdown noise and its screen fades to black. He puts the phone back into the rucksack, zips the rucksack up and puts it on his shoulders.

Hill closes his eyes and listens to the Irish Sea.

He opens his eyes and listens to the Irish Sea.

Hill closes his eyes and listens to the forest.

He opens his eyes and listens to the forest.

Hill remembers going for a walk with Roger in this forest when he was eight. They had the family dog, Jess, with them – a small Labrador Border Collie cross. She was five years old, enthusiastic, needy and emotional. She loved life and eating her own shit. Hill used to talk to Jess and had regular ~30-minute conversations with her, often detailing his plans for the school week and then the weekend. Jess would look back optimistically, as if she were kindly humouring him. During the walk that day, Roger asked Hill what he'd like to do with his life. Hill said he wanted to be an Olympic 100 metre sprinter but Roger suggested he try middle distance running instead. Hill was disappointed and didn't speak for the rest of the walk. He decided it was pointless telling Roger anything like this again and instead would save this kind of talk for his mother. Roger began talking about Sebastian Coe, whom he despised, and Steve Ovett, whom he admired, and didn't stop until they were back at the house. It was a long and boring morning.

Hill begins laughing.

Roger was trolling me, Hill thinks.

is trolling me, Hill thinks.

will always troll me, Hill thinks.

Hill looks up to the sky and carries on laughing.

He begins walking towards the noise in the distance. Moving slowly, cautiously, avoiding any sudden dips in the ground, with his hands out in front of him feeling the way, Hill realises that he is leaving the forest. His feet sink a fraction into the ground as they begin walking on sand.

Tiny plastic comets

Hihihi, you're here! Hill's here! Trudy shouts. She is wearing an oversized navy cable-knit sweater, floral surf shorts, and retro grey Air Max.

There are at least thirty people around a large fire; some of them dancing to drum and bass being played off a portable Bose speaker, some of them sitting on small camping chairs, talking to each other with focused facial expressions. Hill stops walking and immediately feels self-conscious.

Please, a tidal wave, Hill thinks.

Trudy stops dancing and runs over to Hill. She jumps up at him, holding one hand out for a high-five. Hill high fives her and looks at her face for ~10 seconds.

Intense! Trudy laughs. You're really really late, it's fine though. What time even is it? What even time is it? What am I even saying? You want some NOS?

Sure, Hill says.

***

When my phone ran out, I don't know, I just felt like maybe that was actually the best thing that's happened to me in the whole time I've been here, Hill says. It was dark, like truly I couldn't see anything, and it felt possible to think. I remembered my dog's face, and I don't mean generically I recalled what a Collie's face would look like, I actually remembered Jess' face. I hadn't thought of her for years. It felt good connecting with an emotional experience that wasn't also somehow tied to anything that's still relevant today. Then I thought of Roger, which ruined the moment of course. But it felt good overall. Jess, a lovely friend to me. Standing there, in the middle of the forest, in darkness, I probably would have thrown the phone away into the sea if I could throw that far, he says, feeling lightheaded, struggling to focus when not speaking.

Fuck! Let's do that now! Trudy springs to her feet and starts dancing and shouting.

What, no, I don't—

No, no, too late, Trudy says. It's a statement. Let's all do it. Everyone, we're going to throw our phones away! Into the sea! This is Hill's idea!

No, I don't ... my phone is really—

Trudy pulls Hill up by his arms and begins dragging him towards the water. A small group of other people are following; as Hill turns round to look at them he sees their solemn facial expressions – one of them, the MDMA man from the house party, slowly bangs on a small drum that's hanging from his waist by a frayed string belt.

Trudy kicks off her shoes and walks into the sea.

Waaaaaaawooooooo! Fuck you, phone fucker! she screams, delighted.

The small group cheers wildly as Trudy's phone flies out of her hand and into the darkness. The blond man bangs on his drum louder, quicker. Hill looks at him and attempts to smile but instead looks unhinged.

Do I have phone insurance, Hill thinks.

Feel sick, Hill thinks.

The blond man with the drum looks back at Hill and smiles broadly. Your turn, Hill, he says. Everybody! Hill's turn, Hill's turn, Hill's turn, Hill's turn, Hill's turn, Hill's turn.

Fucking do it, Hill! Trudy is grinning, jumping up and down in the water.

Hill slowly opens his rucksack and takes out the phone.

It's just, this is a really expen—

The man on the drum glares at Hill and bangs his drum harder. Throw the phone, bro, he says.

Hill attempts to kick his shoes off, but they're too tight.

I need this, it—

Hill looks at Trudy, beckoning him into the sea, full of enthusiasm.

It has footage of—

Hill walks into the sea wearing his shoes and holding his phone.

He looks at Trudy, who leans in towards him and takes his hands in hers.

Give me the phone and throw this instead, Trudy whispers as she transfers a large pebble into Hill's other hand.

Okay, thank you, I love you, Hill says.

Hill turns to face the ocean and throws the pebble as far as he can. The crowd cheer and begin throwing their phones into the sea. Hill and Trudy look up and see tiny plastic comets, LED-lit shooting stars, fly over their heads. Trudy laughs and whoops. The blond man is still pounding his drum, and continues on the same beat as he and the others make their way back to the campfire.

Trudy puts her hands around Hill's waist and blows a raspberry. Hill looks at Trudy and feels an urge to record her looking directly into camera and responding to questions concerning her life and happiness, questions concerning the island's forests, beaches, and roads, questions concerning other things.

I would have thrown it, Hill says.

Hill and Trudy stand in the water, looking at each other calmly. Trudy leans in towards Hill and kisses him on the lips.

Hill shuts his eyes and listens to the water.

Mixed Lego

Hill takes a long drink from a 550ml carton of Orange and Lime Tropicana and slowly walks up the steep, winding staircase to the third floor. Hill holds the carton up to his mouth, drinks from it again, then rests the empty carton on the floor next to a plastic container filled with mixed Lego. Hill crouches down over the container and picks up an intricate off-plan spaceship.

Remember making this, Hill thinks.

Hill looks at the petrol pump attendant sitting in the central cockpit, expressionless as both its arms point upwards, away from the tiny grey steering wheel. Hill lifts the spaceship above his head and moves it slowly across an imaginary planet and towards a nearby black hole.

Remember making things, Hill thinks.

Hill places the Lego spaceship back in the container and looks down the long, narrow corridor.

Has Trudy ever been up here, Hill thinks.

Hill looks at his phone and refreshes WhatsApp, Gmail, Messenger in rotation for several minutes.

Matthew McConaughey weight-loss journey

Hill stands at the door to Trudy's building. He is holding a six pack of Coors Light and a bag of Co-op porridge oats. The walk from the house to Trudy's flat is 10.5 kilometres and Hill can feel the blisters on his heels throbbing.

Bad choice to walk, Hill thinks.

Too many bad choices, Hill thinks.

Hill looks up at Trudy's window, the light shining through a gap in the curtains.

Am I enjoying this less, Hill thinks.

Will she give me money for the beer and oats, Hill thinks.

Shut up, Hill thinks.

Hill presses the button for Trudy's flat, takes a step backwards and looks up towards her window.

***

Trudy presses pause and the film freezes on Matthew McConaughey and Penélope Cruz lying on a beach, looking into each other's eyes. Matthew McConaughey's character is called Dirk Pitt, Penélope Cruz's character is called Eva Rojas. Dirk Pitt is a 'master explorer and former Navy Seal' and Eva

Rojas is a 'beautiful and brilliant UN scientist'. They didn't get along at the start of the film and now they do get along. Lying next to each other on the beach, everything has worked out well on their unique and perilous adventure. The viewer is naturally ecstatic at this outcome.

So problematic, rampant fucking patriarchy, Trudy says.

Attractive bozos, Hill thinks.

Why are you smiling, Hill? Trudy says.

Films should come with subtitled trigger warnings, Hill says.

Trudy looks angry and gets up to go to the toilet. She shuts the door behind her.

If you can't see the problem with that piece of shit film then we have a major issue, Trudy says over the sound of her peeing. And please don't make fun of trigger warnings.

Hill looks at his phone to check the time. He looks at the projector and follows the light up to the wall. Netflix has automatically reverted to the menu screen, hundreds of incredible viewing options slowly rotating before him.

It makes me consider whether you view anything from the female perspective? Trudy says over the sound of the toilet roll spinning and paper being torn. The toilet flushes and Trudy opens the door and stands there with her hands on her head.

I'm half serious, half joking, I don't know, Trudy says. Why do we watch these films?

We're masochists, because that's the easy thing to be, I think, Hill says. I mean, why am I even here. Not here here, I mean on the island with Roger?

Well, why are you? Trudy says.

I don't know, truly, Hill says. He's a lonely, bitter old man. It's terrifying. Maybe I feel like if I put the time in with him it'll somehow... I don't know.

I don't know what 'put the time in' means in your language, Hill, Trudy says.

Hill picks up a can of Coors Light and takes a small sip. He feels the pressure from his fingers begin to squeeze the can out of shape. Loosening his grip, Hill takes a small sip and then a much longer one.

Roger, Hill thinks.

Hill takes another, much longer drink from the can.

He killed my mother, Hill says.

Trudy squats and puts her head face down in her hands. She looks up at Hill, her eyes wide open, her lips pursed.

Fuck, Hill, that's insane. You can't possibly believe that? Trudy says. She pulls her phone out of her trouser pocket, looks at the screen, and puts it back in the pocket. You don't believe that, she says.

Who was that? Hill says.

It was no one, Trudy says. Answer my question.

Trudy moves over to the futon and lies down next to Hill. She takes the Coors Light from his hand and takes a large gulp and then another large gulp. Hill looks at Trudy and then towards the wall.

Maybe, I think he's vindictive, even if only subconsciously, Hill says. He considers me firstly to be his wife's son. That's always been my understanding. My mother, in her will, left the house to me. Roger is allowed to live there until he dies or chooses to leave. He took that out on me. It wasn't my fault. Maybe it explains a lot, I don't know. What's the difference? I don't think she intended to mean anything by it, other than protect me in case he got married again. But Roger is such a fucking egotist, it killed him.

Trudy runs her hand through her hair, pinning it back as she takes a small sip from the Coors Light.

Roger got older ... ill, Hill says. The emails, endless streams of shit cut and pasted financial growth clickbait, siding with Lucy's parents over her funeral, her ashes, the obsession with converting the clock tower. I don't know, sorry.

Hill finds Sahara and selects the resume watching option.

'Matthew McConaughey weight loss journey', Hill thinks.

Matthew McConaughey weight loss journey, Hill says.

Yeah, great, Trudy says. But don't you think it seems like all of that was Roger's way of saying sorry, trying to help maybe? Seems like his whole life revolves around you.

There is a vibrating sound in the room and Trudy puts her hand over her trouser pocket. The sound still audible, Trudy presses her hand down harder.

Roger doesn't..., Hill says, looking at Trudy's trouser pocket.

Trudy takes the phone out again and looks at the screen. Trudy slides the phone back into her pocket. He doesn't blame you for your mum dying if that's what you think, she says.

Hill stares at the wall and tries to make out individual grains of sand in between Penélope Cruz's toes.

He told me he forgave you for saying you wished he'd died instead of her, Trudy says.

I was fifteen when I said that, Hill says. He's an absolute maniac if he's still—

He told me he forgave you, Hill—

Which obviously means he's still sore over it, Hill says. Which isn't even the point. It's really fine though.

Hill looks at Penélope Cruz's black and white striped swimming cap, her sunglasses, her long nose, her lips.

He'd like it if you could forgive him, Hill, Trudy says.

I think we should watch another problematic film, Hill says.

***

Hill presses the light button on his watch. The time reads 03:30. There is a faint smell of damp in the room, made worse by the radiator having been turned on at full power all evening; Trudy repeatedly promised to turn it off before they fell asleep but evidently hadn't.

Hill looks over to Trudy and she is lying on her front, face pressing into the pillow, arms tight to her sides, her fingers pointing down towards the duvet, half off the bed, the other bunched around her calves and feet.

Hill gets up from the futon and walks over to the radiator, kneeling before it and twisting the radiator valve to the off position. He walks over to the window and prises two of the blind's plastic strips apart. He leans forward and presses his face against the blind. A large fishing boat moves slowly and silently across the water in the direction of the pier. The island is mostly in darkness. Excluding the lights that outline the two bridges, Hill counts five house lights. As Hill moves away from the blind it springs back into position, making a sudden clattering noise. He looks over towards Trudy, still perfectly still, but her left arm now stretched across onto the other side of the bed. Hill presses the light button on his watch. The time reads 03:30.

Hill walks into the kitchenette and over to the fridge. He opens it and puts his hand on the last can of Coors Light. He puts his hand on a one litre plastic carton of oat milk. He puts his hand on an unopened two-litre bottle of Evian. Hill shuts the fridge door.

There is a vibrating sound coming from Trudy's trousers. Hill walks over to her trousers. He looks over towards Trudy. He puts his hand in her trouser pocket. He takes his hand out of her trouser pocket. He walks over to the futon and places the duvet over Trudy so that it covers her from her neck down. Hill lies down on the futon and presses the light button on his watch. The time reads 03:30.

An arresting image

Hill is sitting on an old wrought iron chair. The chair was painted a different colour every summer when Hill was young, something his mother did with all the garden furniture. She didn't stop working during her summer holidays; Hill would sit and watch, try to help where he could, even as a clumsy five-year-old. *You're helping just by being here*, his mother would say, smiling.

Hill looks at the flaking neon green paint on the chair and picks a piece off before flicking it onto the floor.

It's hot, Hill thinks.

Should sunbathe, Hill thinks.

Hill picks up his cup of water from the floor and takes a small sip. He looks at the lawn ahead of him, so even and well maintained. A man in his late sixties works on the garden every other week.

I don't know his name, Hill thinks.

I am the worst person ffs, Hill thinks.

I don't know what time it is, Hill thinks.

Hill looks at the lawn and then looks at his feet. He picks up the cup of water and takes a small sip. Hill looks at his left arm and feels a sudden urge to bite himself very hard.

Don't do it, Hill thinks.

Do it, fuckhead, Hill thinks.

Jack Black, Hill thinks.

Hill thinks about Jack Black's facial expression as he lowers Jack Black headfirst into a volcano. Hill thinks about Jack Black's facial expression as Jack Black searches his name on Twitter and looks at subtweets relating to Gulliver's Travels. Hill thinks about Jack Black's facial expression as a studio intern hands Jack Black a large plate of kale. Hill thinks about Jack Black's facial expression as Jack Black walks aimlessly around his fifteen-million-dollar bungalow.

Just do it, Hill thinks.

Hill moves his arm towards his mouth then hears footsteps behind him. He looks at his arm for a moment then turns around and sees Trudy walking towards him. Trudy is wearing a plain green T-shirt, Chicago Bulls basketball shorts, barefoot. She is carrying a plate of chopped fruits and is biting down on the wooden handle of a small fork. He hasn't seen Trudy for three days and feels an overwhelming sense of relief that she's at the house with him at this moment.

The previous evening Hill watched Bitter Lake by Adam Curtis, as recommended to him by Ed. The reference to Solaris seemed appealing but he felt miserable that Trudy wasn't there with him and gave up halfway through, spending the next hour Googling himself, and then various people from his year at school. He was surprised how little there was online about anyone, how there was probably more about him than all of the rest combined. Hill had fallen asleep thinking about a Russian boy called Maxim who paid the fees in cash every term and insisted that his dad was an arms dealer. Maxim had a haircut like a young Ralph Macchio and used to sit in the sixth form basement eating Chinese noodles and playing Snake on his Nokia. He'd threatened to have someone killed but fifteen years later didn't even have a LinkedIn. Wtf, Maxim, Hill had thought as he drifted off to sleep.

Trudy puts the plate of chopped fruit down on the lawn and pulls a matching wrought iron chair over towards Hill. She sits on the chair and leans forwards, picking up a handful of sliced peach. She eats the peach slices and licks her hands. She looks at the lawn and smiles. She leans forwards and picks up a handful of sliced star fruit. She eats the star fruit slices and licks her hands. She looks at the lawn and smiles. She leans forward and picks up a handful of sliced kiwi. She eats the sliced kiwi and licks her hands. She looks at the lawn and smiles. She leans forward and picks up a handful of sliced pear. She eats the sliced pear and licks her hands. She looks at the lawn and smiles. She leans forward and picks up a handful of sliced strawberries. She eats the sliced strawberries and licks her hands. She looks at the lawn, her eyes focusing on a deflated football.

Ralph is the main doggy doggle, Trudy says.

I finished the fruit, Trudy says.

What have you done so far today, Hill? Trudy says.

Hill and Trudy sit on the wrought iron chairs, one neon pink, the other red, and look at the lawn. Hill looks at Trudy.

I was going to email you a link to a documentary that my friend recommended, Hill says. I watched an hour, it was okay. My main aspiration is to live to see the end of the world. I think this film confirmed that.

Bleak, Trudy says. She unties her hair and leans forward, obscuring her face. She runs her hands along the ground in between her feet and underneath the chair. She presses her hands down hard and feels the rough edges of the slate patio slabs against her fingers and palms.

No, I mean I want to live to see the end of the world and then carry on existing, Hill says. That seems okay. When they blow up the planet in Star Wars, that's an arresting image. It's operatic. Princess Leia watches as her home planet is blown up, she looks angry and upset but it seems to free her. I don't know, maybe, maybe not. The God in Solaris, that's appealing. It's so calm. We're two people sitting on chairs on a lawn. The grass on the lawn is short and well kept. Is this calm? If we walk across the lawn and through the gate we can walk down a path and onto a slipway. We can take our shoes off and stand on the slipway, the water will touch our feet. I wrote you an email but didn't send it, it's in the draft folder.

I'd be interested to read it, Trudy says. Don't send it until it's ready though.

Trudy looks at Hill. Trudy looks away from Hill. A robin lands on the deflated football and stands there momentarily. Hill and Trudy watch as the robin flies from the football towards the rose bush, then to the birdbath, where it parades around the inside edge and repeatedly bobs his head into the rainwater. There is the muffled sound of a phone vibrating. Trudy puts her hand over her trouser pocket, gets up, and walks back into the house.

Hill looks straight ahead and watches as the robin propels itself off the outer edge of the birdbath and upwards into the glare of the midday sun.

Such pain and style

Lying on top of his bed, eyes shut, Hill can hear the sound of radio voices coming from Roger's room and, above that, the intermittent banging of plates, cutlery, and saucepans travelling upstairs from the kitchen.

Never leave this room, Hill thinks.

Hill feels Dave's paw gently press down on his eyelid.

What, Hill says.

Dave lifts his paw and presses it down on Hill's eyelid.

What, Hill says.

Dave lifts his paw and presses it down on Hill's eyelid.

Attempting to help me, somehow, Hill thinks.

Hill gently lifts Dave's paw away from his eyelid and opens his eyes. He looks at Dave, both front paws now tucked in underneath his body, his facial markings perfectly symmetrical but for a thin scar running like a tear from the corner of his left eye down to his cheek.

Dave stares back at Hill, expressionless.

Such pain and style, Hill thinks.

Hill sits up and lifts Dave off his lap, placing him back down on the thick tartan blanket. He watches Dave stand up and walk in circles, each one smaller than the last, before settling down again, tucking his head tightly into his body. Dave's body twitches momentarily before falling perfectly still.

Hill feels under the blanket for his phone, checks the time, then lies back down on the bed and stares up at the cracked ceiling rose.

I used to lie here, Dave, and look at these cracks for hours every Sunday morning, Hill says. These cracks are older than me. They're older than Google. They're probably older than many other things. The time I spent looking, waiting for them to get worse, change. I found it fascinating. I think I enjoyed it. The cracks were either going to get worse or stay the same. It's okay. Don't worry about me. I'm not sure it matters, Davey.

Blue and Yellow Trail Arrows

Hill stops pedalling and lets the bicycle freewheel down the hill, the view over to the mainland gradually receding until he is surrounded by tightly packed pine trees and blue and yellow trail arrows.

How many days since we communicated, Hill thinks.

Hill takes a photo of the bike's front wheel pointing towards a narrow dirt track with the caption: I'm an outdoors guy now. you?

Hill touches *send*, touches *cancel*, and then watches as the message is sent, received, and seen.

Hill turns his phone off and puts it in his trouser pocket. He looks around for red squirrels before pedalling aggressively towards the trail that leads to the water's edge.

TRUDY

You were on TV

Trudy stands in the downstairs hall and watches as Moji, her stepbrother Trystan's cat, walks across her feet and towards his food.

Moji sits in front of the yellow china bowl, overflowing with cat biscuits, and turns his head to Trudy.

Moji stares at Trudy.

Yes Moji, it is weird you have my childhood cereal bowl, Trudy says.

What's mine is ... theirs, Trudy thinks.

What's theirs is ... theirs, Trudy thinks.

COOL! Trudy thinks.

Moji crouches and eats some biscuits, his long, fluffy tail twitching and wafting across the parquet floor. Trudy looks up and sees the plumber walking down the stairs. She watches him rock forward and backwards as he says things about the boiler and then other things relating to the electrical wiring.

It's not a small job, fair play, He says.

It's okay, sure, if you can do the boiler, please, Trudy says.

You were in the year above me at school—

If you know an electrician, or, Trudy says, her hands in her pockets, her fingers pinching her thighs.

You were on TV—

Yes. Thank you, Trudy says. If you know an electrician, or.

New Yurt?? Maybe?

Trudy puts a copy of Good Morning, Midnight face down on the table and picks up her phone.

I'll transfer the money now, Trudy says. Yes ... I did ... I will... Okay. Dad?

'Love you too', Trudy thinks.

Trudy touches her phone and transfers money to her dad, Julian.

Trudy touches her phone, typing and then deleting a message intended for Hill.

Trudy looks at an email with the subject header *New Yurt?? Maybe?* from her mum, Sally.

Too much, Trudy thinks. Fuck off, mum, just—

Trudy touches her phone, typing and then deleting a message intended for Hill.

Trudy picks up Good Morning, Midnight and puts it back down on the table, face down.

Trudy looks at her phone and reads a message from her dad.

Trudy looks at her phone and deletes, unread, a new email from her mum.

Trudy touches her phone, typing and then deleting a message intended for Hill.

A barista brings coffee over to Trudy's table and rests the cup on the metal table top.

An oat flat-white, the barista says.

Thank you, Trudy says, putting Good Morning, Midnight down on the table.

Is everything—

It's great, no, it's, thank you, Trudy says, her fingernails digging into her forearms, her phone flashing with messages from her mum, her dad, drug dealer one, Amazon Prime, Netflix, Pet Plan, drug dealer two, Co-op, others.

Caernarfon Diaz

Drinking straight from the blender cup, Trudy downs a smoothie made from avocado, kale, spinach, cucumber, pear and oat milk. She turns the cup upside down and places it in the sink, next to another upturned blender cup.

Too fast, too furious, Trudy, says to Ralph, her eyes watering.

Ralph walks away from Trudy and jumps onto the armchair next to the bay window.

Okay, Trudy thinks.

Trudy touches her phone, typing and then deleting a message intended for Hill.

Trudy picks up her laptop from the kitchen worktop, clicks play, and listens to Cameron Diaz shout at Al Pacino as she walks out of the kitchen and towards her bed.

Trudy looks at her phone, smiles, and types Caernarfon Diaz–

Trudy looks at her phone and types Oliver Stone you loon–

Trudy looks at her phone and types nothing.

Trudy watches Elizabeth Berkley attempt to solicit Al Pacino.

Trudy watches Jamie Foxx argue with Dan Quaid, LL Cool J, Al Pacino.

Trudy watches Al Pacino shout at Cameron Diaz, Cameron Diaz shout at Arron Eckhart, Dan Quaid shout at Jamie Foxx, Al Pacino talk quietly at first, build to a crescendo, and shout at a large group of men who include among them Jamie Foxx, Dan Quaid, LL Cool J, Arron Eckhart.

Trudy touches her phone, typing and then deleting a message intended for Hill.

Trudy looks at her phone and sets the alarm for 04:55.

Trudy closes her eyes, extends her hands out in front of her and shuts her laptop.

Wait

Trudy lets Ralph off his lead and watches as he runs towards the woodland area to the left of the car park.

Not too far, Trudy says. No, wait. Follow me.

Trudy runs, stops, waits, then runs as Ralph turns and gallops in her direction. The pair run at first on the gravel track leading to the beach, the south stack lighthouse briefly visible on the horizon, then up an embankment and back down into the woodland, running parallel to the beach. The dawn sun is rising. They run together, jumping over exposed tree trunks, nettles, brambles, slowing when they need to, sprinting where they can.

Don't ruin this smoothie for me

Hill moves his index finger over the trackpad and scrolls through the categories.

Violent Revenge Thrillers

Films With Happy Endings

Zany Comedies

Strong Female Leads

Tom Cruise

Films With Sad Endings

Violent Revenge Thrillers

Don't like choosing, Hill thinks.

Don't want Trudy to choose, Hill thinks.

There's nothing, 'literally' nothing, Hill says.

Language evolves, Hill, you literally need to accept that, Trudy says.

Hill looks over towards the kitchenette area of Trudy's flat. She is standing on one foot and chopping up bananas, strawberries, raspberries, passion fruit with a large Global knife. She is wearing a dark green oversized cable-knit sweater, black leggings, barefoot. Her iPhone is resting horizontally against a white toaster, playing music that Hill doesn't recognise.

Who is this? Hill says.

Urgh, Hill thinks.

Do you like it, it's very relevant, Trudy says. She doesn't turn around as she carries on chopping the fruit whilst standing on one foot. She changes foot and shouts, I just beat my single leg record, do you like this music?

I love it, Hill says, trying not to sigh. I want us to choose a film before we have our smoothies. What genre do you want?

Hill looks again at the categories on offer and feels anxious that Trudy will ask for Violent Revenge Thrillers. Hill moves the laptop to the other side of the futon. He looks at his iPhone and sees that Ed is messaging him. Hill puts his iPhone back into his pocket and leans over to pick up the laptop. He looks at the screen.

Jason Statham, Hill thinks.

Liam Neeson, Hill thinks.

Era of Most Violent Revenges, Hill thinks.

Jack Black, Hill thinks.

Hill looks over towards Ralph. Ralph is asleep in his basket, snoring.

I hate you, Hill thinks.

Nope, don't mean that, Hill thinks.

Trudy walks over to the futon and sits down, passing Hill a half-filled glass of fruit smoothie. Don't you wish we could spend all our time in here, watching films and drinking smoothies? Trudy says. Imagine what we'd learn about ourselves.

I know probably everything there is to know about myself, Hill says.

Jesus, Hill thinks.

I honestly just thought, Trudy says, laughing. No, nothing.

Trudy leans over and takes the smoothie glass from Hill's hand and drinks it all. Fuck that's good, she says. I really think we should do some more filming, like make a film film. What's stopping us? Did you read that Mark Duplass interview I emailed you?

Hill looks at the Netflix menu.

Are you going to respond to me, Trudy says. Don't ruin this smoothie for me. I think it's ridiculous how you punish yourself. If you don't do the things you love—

What? Hill says.

If you don't do the things you love or make you feel good, then that's self-harm, Trudy says. If you read about it, and I've read about it, you'll see that that is actually what self-harm is, and you're doing it, she says, her hand gesticulating wildly but awkwardly, like a bird learning to fly.

Do you want to watch a film with Jason Segel in it? Hill says. I read a review that said his performance in Sex Tape was haunting, that he starved himself to try and look like a leading man, that you can see his pain and self-loathing in every scene. That's entertainment isn't it? I first watched it on an aeroplane, I couldn't take my eyes off him.

Hill, please, Trudy says. Please try and relax, please try and talk to me like you're comfortable in my company. It's not that I don't want to know, um, Jesus, I mean, let's enjoy these smoothies. Let's enjoy just sitting here.

Trudy finishes drinking from the smoothie glass, tilts it up and waits for the remaining smoothie to drip into her mouth. Hill looks at her neck, long and pale. Hill looks at her hair, long and blonde. Hill watches as the smoothie drips into her mouth bit by bit.

Trudy picks a small piece of pulped strawberry out of the glass and puts it in her mouth.

Most Beautiful Suicide Method

The Volvo starts on the first attempt, a rare and unsettling event. Hill curses and revs the engine loudly over and over. He looks up towards Roger's bedroom and revs again, even louder, attempting to blow the engine.

Conceding defeat, Hill puts the car into second and turns it to face the driveway.

***

The journey off the island is broken up by two traffic delays, both seen as signals by Hill that he shouldn't go through with the school visit.

Once on the mainland, the journey to Rose College is an unpunctuated twenty-minute drive along a grey dual carriageway that runs adjacent to the Irish Sea.

Hill picks a cassette at random from the glove compartment and puts it in the player.

Hill puts the car into fifth and looks straight ahead as Do They Know It's Christmas? begins playing through the one working speaker.

***

Hill parks the car beneath the large Rose College sign and

immediately feels weak and nauseous. Planted deep into a vibrant, immaculate lawn, the billboard projects the Rose College crest and school's Latin motto out towards Colwyn Bay; a permanent, belligerent IMAX for the town's inhabitants.

TrUtH, kNoWleDgE, fAiTh™, Hill thinks.

Hill gets out of the car and begins walking towards the main reception. The email said that Hill would be met by the head of the English department.

Sweating, Hill thinks.

McCarthy, Hill thinks.

Nope, Hill thinks.

Hill turns around to walk back to the Volvo. He doesn't want to do this. He doesn't need the money; this week, today, right this instant, he doesn't need the money. He has enough money on him to drive to a supermarket and buy discounted packet sandwiches. Hill wants to buy a packet ploughman's sandwich, a packet cheese and onion sandwich, a packet egg and mayo sandwich, and eat them one after the other in a large supermarket car park. Hill wants to finish eating them and then carefully fold the empty packets into each other to make one tightly packed empty packet before returning to the supermarket to buy more. This process will be repeated indefinitely.

Most beautiful suicide method, Hill thinks.

As Hill turns, he hears a voice calling him. A girl in a dark pinstriped trouser suit is saying his name. She is tall and has long

145

dark hair with highlights. She walks over to Hill and introduces herself as Molly Edwards-Jones, Head Girl. She has four gold badges on the lapels of her suit jacket and small piercing holes on her right eyebrow and down the side of her right ear. Her skin is clear and her teeth are straight apart from the middle tooth on the bottom row which cuts across somewhat.

McCarthy can't come, Molly says. He's, *something*, I don't know what.

Great, sure, thank you, Hill says.

It's amazing you're here, Molly says. Your Instagram is properly dry, haha. I have to give you a tour of the new astroturf or something. Make you aware of our alumni donation appeal?

Oh, great, Hill says.

Hill and Molly begin walking through the quad and up the concourse. The astroturf is made up of three large pitches, overlooked by a glass-fronted pavilion, and behind that a large newly-built classroom block. Molly is talking about her parents forcing her to stay in Dubai over the summer when a Boost wrapper blows across the ground towards them.

Don't, Hill thinks.

Hill bends over to pick the wrapper up.

Just Done It™, Hill thinks.

Hill looks around for a bin. They are walking across the middle of the astroturf, there are no bins anywhere.

Don't do it, Hill thinks.

Hill puts the Boost wrapper in his pocket and squeezes it, digging and grinding his fingernails into the palm of his hand.

Beyond redemption now, Hill thinks.

Buy ten of these after, Hill thinks.

Eat until you die, Hill thinks.

He looks towards Molly, now talking on her phone.

Molly puts her phone in her jacket pocket and stops walking. She faces Hill and puts her hand on his arm. This must be so boring for you? she says, grinning. This whole place is really, really awful. Do you wakeboard?

***

Hill finishes talking to the group of English students, smiles, and pretends to make a note in his diary as they clap enthusiastically, their apparent sincerity catching him off-guard. It's the same classroom that Hill was in for his English A Level and hasn't changed much; the thin wooden tables, posters for Titus Andronicus, Death of a Salesman, Macbeth, the single-glazed stained window panes, albeit the wooden frames now restored. Hill looks towards the corner table where he used to sit next to Clemmy. A girl with braces is sitting there, her eyes closed and facial expression neutral and calm. Her fingers are miming playing the piano.

What the fuck, Hill thinks.

The students begin asking questions, one after the other, a relentless quest for truth and information.

What are you currently working on?

What do you like to experience outside of work and does this inform your output?

Has the trade-off between a large studio and Jack Black's indie meant a more intimate experience?

Do you wakeboard?

How big a part do you think Rose College has played in your success?

Do you offer an internship?

What do you believe is the relationship, if any, between, but not limited to, the artist's need to tell the profound truth and or deliver entertainment to the intended audience?

Will you ever tweet again?

Do you wakeboard?

Do you wakeboard?

Is it true you took Mr McCarthy's house bell in Norton and mailed him photos of it in various locations? [Uproarious laughter] If so [laughter still going], if so [laughter increasing], if so, what tips would you give for anyone wanting to do something similar in the future? [Uproarious laughter].

The pupil asking this question is a boy with short, side-parted hair and clear braces. He is wearing a light grey pinstriped suit and has a new-looking copy of Atlas Shrugged in front of him on his desk, the book's spine facing Hill. Hill looks down beneath the desk and sees a large iPhone propped up in landscape against the boy's belt, its unblinking lens and cracked fascia seeming wildly menacing.

The boy is staring at Hill, waiting for an answer.

Hill forces a smile and pretends to make a note in his diary.

***

Hill sits in the driver's seat of the Volvo and looks ahead at the car parked in front of him, an Audi A1 with the number plate M0LLY ED and a *Love, Laugh, Live, Wakeboard* sticker in the bottom corner of the rear window.

Molly... Clemmy... Dubai, Hill thinks.

Families That Rose College Together..., Hill thinks.

Hill sees his phone flash with an email from Roger.

He looks up towards the third floor of Central Block and the ornate stained-glass windows that run across the length of the English department.

Where was McCarthy, Hill thinks.

Hill puts the car into second, revving the engine violently as he pulls out onto the road and away from Rose College.

There's still time (an email)

Hill! I'm going to shock, astound and delight you.

Brace yourself, but I think you were right about dairy. The information is out there, and I have found it. There are documentaries that will blow your mind if they have not already done so.

Did you know that the actor Joaquin Phoenix is a based vegan, vegan based, or however you say it? We saw him in Gladiator together, he was terrific if I recall correctly. We shouldn't have stopped going to the cinema. Well. Hill, if we could just

Am emailing Trudy a new shopping list by the way. Down with dairy! Only Oatly! I'm ready to live on in this brave new world with you all. There's still time Hill, what do you think?

There's always time (a reply to an email)

There's always time.

Send me the list, I'll stop at Co-op on the way home.

VNVBFOJDOSJDOJDOHKHJFJD

Did you think about hooking up with Molly? Trudy says. She is sitting on the floor beneath the bay window of her apartment, grinning, rolling a small joint. Should I get an undercut?

I hate that, 'hooking up', it's dreadful, Hill says.

What, why? Actually, no, whatever. But did you think about it? Trudy says. She picks up a bag of weed and holds it underneath her nose. You definitely did think about it, she says.

I did not. Are you trying to cancel me? Hill says.

You didn't answer about whether I should get an undercut? Trudy says. She passes the joint to Hill and blows the smoke towards the open window. She is wearing a large green parka over a vintage Disneyland T-shirt and black leggings. I think you're getting bored of me, it's okay, we haven't committed to anything, she says.

Trudy's phone lights up and she stands and takes it with her to the bathroom. Hill stubs the joint out and looks over towards Ralph, asleep in his basket, and then at the Netflix menu screen on the laptop. He clicks on the search bar and hovers his fingers over the keyboard. He types FILM then holds down the delete button.

He types MOVIE then holds down the delete button.

He types FEATURE LENGTH MOTION PICTURE then holds down the delete button.

He types TELL ME A FILM TO WATCH then holds down the delete button.

He types LITERALLY ANY FILM then holds down the delete button.

He types CHFHGJDUSOFOJDSHFBVCNXNXO then holds down the delete button.

He types VNVBFOJDOSJDOJDOHKHJFJD then holds down the delete button.

I'm going to edit the stuff we shot, Hill says.

Okay, that's good, Trudy says. She flushes the toilet and walks back into the room.

You should choose something, I can't find anything, Hill says. He picks up a can of Red Stripe and drinks one third. I don't understand what you mean when you say we haven't committed to anything.

Jason Statham

Jason Statham's character

'Jason Statham character'

The load screen is frozen on ninety-eight per cent, Jason Statham's facial expression seems hopelessly optimistic next to that of the murdered man slumped against the counter of a Florida swamp bar. Forty-five minutes into this film, Jason Statham has worn a beige and yellow trucker cap in almost every scene. The trucker cap represents his character's desperate struggle for a quiet life; the murdered man represents the right to defend oneself.

Jason Statham, Hill thinks.

Jason Statham's character, Hill thinks.

'Jason Statham character', Hill thinks.

Jason Statham's main adversary in this film is played by James Franco. The makeup department on this film have been instructed to make James Franco appear less attractive than he does in his other films. The audience are being actively dissuaded from siding with James Franco, his face and hair look unwashed and greasy, and his clothes appear grimy. James Franco is saying words like crystal and darling in a deep-south accent and it's clear that his destiny is to be killed by Jason Statham. Jason Statham is an American man who says words like justice and daughter in a south-east London accent and it's clear that his destiny is to kill James Franco and resume his peaceful existence.

The small red circle with ninety-eight per cent displayed in the centre continues to spin. Trudy's flat is cold, she had previously told Hill that her landlord was away for six months and wouldn't return any of her emails.

I think he can definitely see these emails I'm sending, Trudy says. Seems like he doesn't care. I guess maybe it's okay to experience living without heat. I don't know, is he trolling me?

I'm going to start working out, seriously, Hill says. Maybe he's trolling you, it's possible.

Hill looks towards Trudy, she has an angry facial expression. Hill looks back towards the screen and stares at the frozen loading symbol.

Okay, great, Trudy says.

Trudy gets up from the futon and walks into the kitchenette where she opens the tap and pours a small glass of water. Trudy lifts the small glass to her mouth and drinks the water. She holds the glass underneath the tap and pours another glass.

***

The Jason Statham film is seventy minutes in and many people have died or been severely injured. Jason Statham's daughter remains in serious danger, and there is an implication that if she is caught by James Franco and his gang she will be raped, murdered, her body probably buried somewhere in the swamp.

Trudy picks up her phone and walks into the bathroom. She pulls down her leggings and pants and sits on the toilet. Hill pauses the film.

Don't bother pausing, Trudy says.

I'll pause it, Hill says.

You don't need to, I'm not enjoying it, Trudy says.

I'll pause it, I need to go after you, Hill says. Hill clicks pause and listens to Trudy pee. The screen is frozen on a close-up of James Franco with an aggressive facial expression.

No more pee sound, Hill thinks.

Will she flush, Hill thinks.

Hill looks past the laptop screen and towards the window. It's dark outside, the few streetlights on the road beneath the building are obscured by large unkempt trees. Standing on tiptoes, Hill can just about see the strait and the island. Trudy's flat is directly opposite a mansion on the island that was converted to a nursing home in the 1980s, but is now a luxury hotel with a wine tasting cellar and helipad. It was reported that John Major and his wife Norma had stayed there recently.

Thumbs up, would recommend, Hill thinks.

Hill looks towards the half-shut bathroom door and can hear the sound of Trudy's fingers tapping on her phone screen. Who are you messaging? Hill says.

No one, Trudy says. Just some guy. He keeps asking me out.

Okay, Hill says.

Fuck you, Hill thinks.

Hill shuts his eyes.

Don't think about Trudy, Hill thinks.

Don't think about Lucy, Hill thinks.

Don't think about Roger, Hill thinks.

Don't think about anything, Hill thinks.

Hill gets up from the bed and puts his shoes on. He walks over to the desk and pauses as he notices a hand-drawn calendar with *Countdown to Aus* written on it. Hill picks up his wallet and car keys. He looks at the wallet, a gift from Lucy.

Converted me to wallets, Hill thinks.

Legacy, Hill thinks.

Still typing, Hill thinks.

Leave quietly, Hill thinks.

Hill looks over towards the bathroom, the laptop screen, the window, then back towards the bathroom. He walks towards the apartment door, opens it and walks out into the communal hallway and down the wide, twisting oak staircase.

I have to return some videotapes m8 (pt1/2)

Hill pulls over into a lay-by and turns off the car engine. He can feel something digging into him, a broken spring on the car seat perhaps. He takes his phone out of his pocket to check whether Trudy has called.

Trudy has not called.

He stares at Messenger and begins to type.

Hill: Hi big soup

Ed: Hi m8. Your dad sent me another email

Hill: ffs

Ed: Okay

Hill: Okay

Ed: I just think if you want to speak to me you should

Hill: Okay

Ed: About anything

Hill: Okay

Ed: Be quick. I have to return some videotapes m8

Hill: Okay. I too have videotapes to return

Ed: Casual men casually referencing

Hill. Okay

Ed: Okay, fine. Quorn burger, tell me: are you happy, are you an unknowable automaton, are you too sensitive, are you constantly second guessing yourself, are you intermittently and mostly resentfully displaying empathy, are you hurting, are you neutral, are you trying to feel okay, are you thinking about Lucy, are you bored of or by the carer, are you drinking, are you eating, are you feeling a long term, medium term and or impending sense of loss, are you wondering about inheritance, are you obsessively thinking about all the many many injustices you have faced during your difficult difficult life? Are you at the very least making some kind of effort to exist? That last one is important, please answer.

Hill: Big bugle, thank you for your direct and genuine concern. Trudy makes me do things and go places – the time spent thinking of reasons not to do these things and go these places is time I would probably spend thinking about Lucy. Maybe I need to spend this time thinking about Lucy. Yes... Trudy's friends are awful. The houseparties. The... none of this is Trudy's fault. She's got a lot of money from when she was on TV and hasn't bought me a fucking thing the whole time we've spent together. Shit. Can you, me, or anyone handle this kind of truth. Again: None of this is Trudy's fault. She's very intelligent but at times she's ridiculous. 'Same bro, same.' The stuff we've filmed seems okay, she has good comic timing. I'm awful, so wooden and uptight. Nice re: the aesthetic though. I miss us talking about 'the aesthetic'. She loves Roger. Roger.

He'll have told you what's happening to him, probably in the most minuscule and boring detail. He's in pain a lot of the time. I mean, I can hear him at night, revelling in it, any pain he can transfer onto me though, it's great, fine, I'll take it. I don't know, it seems so performative. But. He's trying. He wants to live. He wants

Ed: Yes, he does. He wants to live. He's funny and perceptive. Give him some credit. I like him. I like you!

Hill: Casual white men tearing down the barriers, getting real with each other once and for all...

Ed: Enjoying this piping hot tough love?

Hill: Well. The stuff I filmed with Trudy is

Ed: Edit it, make something, but send it to me please

Hill: Okay I will

Ed: Okay

Hill: Okay

Ed: Okay. Tell me that everything is fine

Hill: I have to return some videotapes m8

Ed: Return those tapes, I'll be here when you get back

Email drafts written whilst listening to real life 'ambient rain on car roof noise' at 3:30-3:45AM

Hi Jack,

I recently re-watched SEX TAPE and felt compelled to email. Your cameo, unexpected as it was, on point, absorbing, achingly truth filled, brought to mind kghjgl;kjhj khl'j'k;ljljljkgghjkh;l khljkl;j;lj;jhjhglkjhl;j;lkh;jhjjh.

Email Sent to Jack Black whilst listening to real life 'ambient rain on car roof noise' at 3:30-3:45AM

Dear 'Jack'

I want to say thank you for showing an interest in my work, truly a great compliment and something that has kept me in good spirits over the last eighteen months that I have been waiting, at great personal cost and through the darkest moments imaginable, for something to happen.

How many times have you watched my film? A good many times I imagine, seeing as you are so enthusiastic to develop it and bring it to a 'whole new audience'. What's your favourite part? Specifically, and in detail. I'm looking for precision in your analysis, Jack.

In absolute concrete terms what direction do you want to take the project in? 'You' said that television was your 'vision' (I can only assume that 'you' are 'relating' your 'vision' to me in an 'accurate manner'?) In this context, and citing clearly defined examples, what exactly is 'your' 'vision'? I'm keen to hear you tell me this. Perhaps we can arrange a Skype for some time in the next seven to ten days? I am currently looking after my father at his house (he is very ill) and as such can speak with you 'at the drop of a hat'. When is 'good' for 'you', 'Jack'?

Have you ever had to deal with a terminally ill person, 'Jack'? Unlike, or like – I guess it's subjective, your films, it's not a 'barrel of laughs'. It's 'really fucking awful'. Roger is not going to 'make it through this', this is one 'battle' that he is not going to 'win'. What was/is your father like? Is he 'belligerent'? Is he 'for all intents and purposes' the 'reason' your mother died? Has he 'skewered' your 'world view' 'seemingly permanently'? Does he 'suck'? Do we have this 'in common'? I'm trying to find 'commonality' between us, so you can maybe 'go the extra mile' towards putting some 'concrete steps' in place to make my life 'better'. I have less money today than the day we Skyped. Is that 'bittersweet' for me? Well, perhaps it is, 'Jack'. You will have more money now than the day we Skyped because of 'sound investments' and a 'great team' 'behind you'. Maybe we can talk about it when we Skype in the next 'seven to ten days'?

All I ever wanted was money, success, happiness. Was that 'too much to ask' hahahahahahhahahahahaahaahhaa. I'm so sad hahahahahahahaha. I look forward to our Skype hahahahahaha

Hahahahahaha,

Hill

I have to return some videotapes m8 (pt2/2)

Hill looks at the phone screen and puts the phone down on the passenger seat. It's started raining heavily, making it difficult to see much through the windscreen. It's dark outside and Hill remembers how he used to walk along this road as an eighteen-year-old when he couldn't afford a taxi back from the pub. On one of these nights he witnessed an accident, a car had hit a kerb, flipped, and split itself in two on a tree. As an ambulance, fire engine, and several police cars arrived, Hill hid in a bush on the other side of the road and watched for two hours as they dragged bodies and body parts out of the wreckage. When Hill arrived home later that night, shaking and staggering from room to room, he saw light escaping from underneath Roger's study door. As he began turning the door handle he heard the sound of Roger quietly crying. Hill let go of the door handle and walked upstairs to his room and lay quietly on his bed, awake, until the morning.

Above the sound of the rain, now torrential, Hill hears the sound of the phone vibrating.

Probably Jack, Hill thinks.

Probably Trudy, Hill thinks.

Hill picks the phone up and reads texts from Domino's:

Hello Friend We Missed You

Hello Friend We Missed You

Hello Friend We Missed You

Hello Friend We Missed You comes through another ~ten times in quick succession before Hill puts the phone back on the passenger seat, facing down.

Hello Friend We Missed You, Hill thinks.

Hill reaches underneath the passenger seat and pulls out Roger's MacBook. He takes it out of the tweed case and opens the screen, the light illuminating the cabin's filthy plastic dashboard and watermarked ceiling. He opens Final Cut Pro and clicks on A Quiet Island. Hill clicks play and the video freezes instantaneously, the cursor turning into a small, perpetually spinning rainbow.

, Hill thinks.

, Hill thinks.

, Hill thinks.

Hill closes his eyes, tunes in to the sound of the rain battering the car, and passes out.

Wakeboarding (A Quiet Island)

A Mastercraft X46 moves through the middle arch of the smaller suspension bridge. A man with short, bleached hair holds the steering wheel and screams loudly, turning and pointing to the man sitting in the back of the boat and then towards the woman on the wakeboard being towed behind it. Once through the arch, the man holding the steering wheel makes a sharp turn towards the mainland, causing the woman on the wakeboard to drive towards the island, lose her balance, and crash into the water. The man holding the steering wheel screams loudly, turning and pointing towards the man sitting in the back of the boat and then towards the woman floating in the water. The man holding the steering wheel powers the boat down and reaches into the fridge for two Desperados.

The woman on the wakeboard floats on her back, her wakeboard pointing upwards. She has sponsorship from a wetsuit company, she has forty-nine thousand followers on Instagram. She lies on her back, floating, looking at the clear sky above her.

The waves from the wipeout have made their way to the shore. A man fishing off the edge of a small green casts his line out into the strait. He is wearing a black Adidas sweater, pale blue jeans, and an old pair of cream Reebok Classics. He works in the island's largest abattoir electrocuting animals and slitting their throats, he has eight-year-old twin girls, he has a motocross bike, he has other things. The man fishing off the edge of a small green casts his line out into the strait and looks up at the clear sky above him.

The man holding the wheel of the Mastercraft finishes the Desperado and screams loudly as he pulls down hard on the throttle and hovers his finger over the brake release button. He turns and points towards the man sitting in the back, and then towards the woman on the wakeboard.

The man fishing off the edge of the small green looks towards the Mastercraft and reels his line in. He looks down into the bucket next to his feet. A dead bass looks back up at him, blood coagulated around its gills.

The wakeboarder looks up at the clear sky above her. She feels the power of the Mastercraft pull her up into a standing position and smiles, her teeth large, white, and incredibly beautiful.

Night Swimmer (A Quiet Island)

A man in his late twenties stands on the shore and looks out towards the sporadically-lit mainland opposite him. He is wearing a seven-millimetre Billabong wetsuit, Neoprene gloves, hood, and Petyl headtorch. Hail is falling, bouncing off his body and onto the rocks and seaweed by his feet.

A red fishing boat moves very slowly across the water. The crew is made up of men between the ages of sixteen and fifty-eight; they sit in the cabin and drink bottles of Carlsberg, every one of them exhausted and stinking, each one reluctantly taking his turn to get up, move to the front of the boat, and navigate them back to the pier.

The sixteen-year-old boy is up in the cabin, holding the wheel, feeling dizzy from three Carlsbergs. The man in the swimsuit's headtorch having caught his eye, the boy looks to shore and waves hopelessly from inside the cabin as he holds down the fishing boat's horn.

The man in the wetsuit waits for the fishing boat to pass, and then for the waves it generates to hit the shore. He looks up towards the suspension bridge, its reflection bearing down on the water, lit by the automated night lights under each archway.

He smiles as he begins walking into the water. After three steps the water is up to his knees.

He looks again at the bridge, the sound of the cars muffled by his hood, and then towards the mainland.

He clasps his hands above his head, dives in, and begins to swim.

One thousand sheets at any given time

The cleared space in the clock tower has enough room for a large desk, a fridge, a futon, and an armchair. The electricity is okay, the internet is patchy. Hill only ever really needs to return to the house to prepare food and use the bathroom.

Hill finishes sorting through the bags of his mother's stuff, most of the clothes still in good enough condition to take to the charity shop. Amongst the bags of fancy dress and laminated teaching resources, there is a small wooden box with his mother's initials and date of birth carved on the top. The box is locked. Hill walks over to the clothes rail and places the box underneath it, next to an unopened bag of cat biscuits and a stack of printer paper; one of Roger's fixations had been to maintain a backup supply of at least one thousand sheets at any given time.

Hill looks at the box, the printer paper, his watch. He puts on a pair of Nike Vomeros, calls Ralph from his basket, and walks outside to complete his morning sprint training.

Somehow a most beautiful image

Hill looks at his watch. It's still dark outside, the wind and rain rattling the two small windows in the downstairs area of the clock tower. It's cold. Hill is wearing an old baseball cap he found in one of his mother's fancy-dress bags, two T-shirts on top of one another, and a cable-knit sweater that Trudy left at the house. He texted her to say that it was there, that she could collect it before she left for Australia, but she didn't respond.

Hill looks at the taupe armchair. Ralph is sitting on it, asleep, snoring. The armchair was in one of the spare bedrooms in the house. Hill tries to remember whether his mother reupholstered it. Hill tries to remember the last conversation he had with his mother. Hill tries to remember the last conversation he had with Trudy; something about Trudy leaving her Nespresso machine with Roger as a loan until she returned from Australia. Hill lies down on the futon and looks up towards the planks of wood that constitute the ceiling. He looks at Dave on the opposite pillow, asleep. He looks at his watch. He looks up towards the planks of wood. Hill gets up from the futon and walks over to the Nespresso machine. He looks at the red and black design then runs his hand over the casing and looks at the unopened boxes of Nespresso pods next to it. He looks at his watch. Hill walks over towards the Wi-Fi router underneath the desk. The smiley face on the router is flashing. Hill picks up the router and the smiley face lights up. He puts the router on the windowsill. The smiley face stays lit. Hill looks at his watch. Everything is fine.

She'll know, Hill thinks.

Hill walks over to the desk and sits down on the chair. He presses the MacBook touchpad, looks at a freeze frame image of a wakeboarder waving at a nearby dolphin, minimises Final Cut Pro. He moves the cursor over the Skype icon. He moves the cursor over the contacts list. He moves the cursor over Trudy Dafis. He looks at the screen and listens to the ringing noise.

No one there... hang up... oh, Hill thinks.

The call connects and Trudy's face appears on screen. Her hair is short, blonder. Her skin is tanned, not darker necessarily, a golden colour. Trudy stares out from the screen, unblinking. She tries to say hi two or three times but breaks down in tears with each attempt, covering her mouth with one hand and her eyes with the other.

Jesus, Trudy says, finally. When did it happen?

Four days ago, Hill says.

Hill looks on as Trudy begins crying. She is clasping her arms around her chest. Hill looks at her arms. She has a small mandala tattoo on her right arm, with something written underneath that he can't make out. She's wearing a Casio, one of Roger's stockpile that he gave her to help with timekeeping. Her arms are tanned and more muscular than before. She is still crying, shaking her head a little and mumbling something over and over.

I can't hear you, Hill says.

Trudy tries to compose herself. She runs her hands through her hair and places them on the table. She clenches her jaw and nods her head. She clasps her hands tightly.

I just wish I'd been there, Trudy says, immediately starting to shake and cry again. She wipes her nose and then wipes her hand on the table in front of her.

Don't know, Hill thinks.

Don't say anything, Hill thinks.

Trudy is looking directly into camera, biting her bottom lip. Her arms are outstretched and she appears to be holding both sides of her laptop screen.

I just want, I don't know, Hill, I just want—

Trudy's voice begins to break up, her image on the screen moving erratically. Hill looks at the Wi-Fi router, the smiley face flashing. Hill gets up from the table and walks over to the small black box. He takes it down from the windowsill and places it on the floor. The smiley face lights up.

Can you hear me, are you listening, Hill? Trudy says.

Yes, my internet is bad, Hill says. I'm here. I didn't hear any of that. Was it important?

Jesus, Hill, Trudy says, simultaneously laughing and crying.

Hill looks at his watch. Hill looks at the ceiling. Hill looks at Dave. Hill looks at Ralph. Hill looks at his running shoes. Hill looks at the wooden box underneath the clothes rail. Hill looks at the screen: Trudy is sitting bolt upright, her eyes red, her mouth open.

Hill, your fucking dad died, say something, Trudy says, the failing internet connection rendering her words a glitchy staccato.

Roger died four days ago, Hill says. I don't know what else to say. He left me instructions on how to do everything. It's okay.

Hill listens to the sound of ancient plumbing briefly shuddering to life, the sound of dog snores, the sound of

I remember the day you left, Hill says. Roger told me he paid for your taxi to the airport. I was so angry. Seems an absurd reaction now. Of course. I don't know. I took Ralph to Llanddwyn the day after you left, he did a shit in the Irish Sea. Friends of yours from the beach party stood and watched him poo but they got angry with me instead. Like I had told him to do it. Of course. It's fine, I consider Ralph my son now.

Hill listens to the sound of dog snores, the sound of a Hudl powering down, the sound of

I emailed Lucy's parents about the ashes, Hill says. You were right, Roger was right, Ed was right, Russell Brand Instagram was right. I don't know. Grief is a journey, self-pity a destination bleep-bleep, bloop-bloop, blah-blah. It's true though. I hope you're happy my friend. That's all I can possibly say.

Hill looks towards the Wi-Fi router, the smiley face staring back towards him, empty and lifeless. He looks up at the screen,

Trudy's face and upper body frozen and heavily pixilated, silent, somehow a most beautiful image.

Hill puts the iPhone down on the table and looks at the wooden box underneath the clothes rail, a small splintering of wood on the side of the box where he prised it open with a screwdriver. The wooden box has paper and photographs inside it. The pieces of paper are carefully folded, the photographs have the date and location written on the back in blue ink. Two photographs are held together by a paperclip. In the first photograph, Hill's mother and Roger are at a restaurant or dinner party maybe. They are sitting next to each other in the central seats of a long L-shaped table. Roger is wearing a dark suit and blue-and-white floral pattern silk tie. Hill's mother is wearing an Asian-influenced turquoise dress. Roger is holding a glass of whisky and a cigarette. Hill's mother is holding a glass of white wine and a cigarette. Roger is in conversation with the man sitting next to him. Hill's mother is in conversation with the woman sitting next to her.

In the second photograph, Hill's mother and Roger are at a restaurant or dinner party maybe. They are sitting next to each other in the central seats of a long L-shaped table. Roger is wearing a dark suit and blue-and-white floral pattern silk tie. Hill's mother is wearing an Asian-influenced fitted turquoise dress. Roger is holding a glass of whisky and a cigarette. Hill's mother is holding a glass of white wine and a cigarette. As the other people in the photo hold their raised their glasses and look towards the photographer, Roger and Hill's mother look at each other, smiling and alive.

Hill minimises Skype and maximises Final Cut Pro.

175

Hill minimises Final Cut Pro and maximises Skype, hovering the cursor over the call button.

Hill minimises Skype, gets up from the chair, and puts on his running shoes.

Six days ago

(Any kind of hope is beautiful)

Hill parks the car in the lay-by and turns the engine off. The radio seems loud now and he turns the volume down. He can still just about hear the English voices talking about whether all human beings are hardwired to be hypocritical. One of the voices states that the moment you acknowledge the concept of hypocrisy, you immediately become a hypocrite. Another voice disagrees with this viewpoint. The original voice repeats his original statement but this time adds 'by disagreeing, you are proving my point' at the end of the sentence.

What, Hill thinks.

What, Hill thinks.

What, Hill thinks.

Hill looks at the dashboard and sees that the air conditioning is set to twenty-nine degrees. He feels his T-shirt sticking to his back.

Will be itchy later, Hill thinks.

Salt water swim, Hill thinks.

Hill considers taking off his padded lumberjack shirt. He considers taking off his padded lumberjack shirt, his T-shirt, his shoes, his socks, his trousers, his pants, and leaving the car, leaving the car and running, screaming, down the pathway beneath the lay-by and jumping into the water. He tries to imagine how many people have drowned in the strait that separates the island from the mainland. He remembers his mother telling him that her father used to swim in the strait, that he had an encyclopaedic knowledge of the various currents. Hill has seen photographs of his grandfather, six foot five inches and blond with a large rectangular block for a head and broad shoulders.

Taliesin the Übermensch, Hill thinks.

The windows are starting to steam up. Hill turns switches in a variety of directions and gradually the windscreen clears. It's hotter still inside the car. Hill turns the radio volume back up. Hill looks straight ahead.

We'll stay for a while, Hill says.

Hill closes his eyes. Hill feels a bead of sweat running down his back, in between his shoulders. He has been working out a lot lately, mainly in the courtyard to the side of the house. His shoulders are noticeably bigger, mainly from press-ups. The squats have made his thighs harder and his bum more muscular. He found Roger's set of kettle bells in one of the small cluster of sheds near the clock tower and they have made his biceps, triceps, pectoral and chest muscles more defined. Hill exercises for an hour every morning, usually between seven and eight, and then runs for between forty and forty-five minutes. Sometimes he does interval sprint training up and down the driveway, other times he runs through the wooded area of the grounds. When doing the sprint training, Hill listens to 90s gangster rap on his old iPod. When running through the woods, Hill listens to 90s gangster rap on his old iPod. The running has led to a reduction in overall body fat and Hill's face has hollowed out like a professional athlete. He has improved his diet by cutting out refined sugar and alcohol. He has implemented portion control and eats pasta far less frequently. Hill's skin is clearer and his teeth are whiter.

Used to eat so much pasta, Hill thinks.

This is real, Hill thinks.

This is real, Hill thinks.

Hill opens his eyes and looks at the water, the bridge, the water, the mountains, the trees, the water, the mountains, the snow, the trees, the water, the fields, the trees, the path, the water, the snow, the trees, the bridge, the mountains, the snow, the mountains, the trees, the shore, the water, the shore, the fields, the path, the mountains. The mountains on the mainland seem closer than Hill remembers them being. He is sure that they're at least twenty miles away, he feels as if he knows this to be factually accurate. He feels in his trouser pocket for his iPhone but can't bring himself to take it out and Google. The snow at the top of the mountain peaks looks perfectly white and this makes him smile. He imagines what it would be like to be up there now, lying in the snow at the top of the mountain, feeling very cold and calm. Hill looks straight ahead. The trees towards the shore on the other side of the strait are tall and dense. Hill can see three or four rooftops of large houses poking out in more landscaped areas. The trees are old and strong. The trees are green and brown and so sure of themselves in the landscape. Hill smiles and looks straight ahead. The shore on the other side of the strait is made up of rocks and seaweed, one or two stone-built boathouses. Hill and his friend Kier used to cycle over to the boathouses and play in them, pretending they were the Bat Cave or tunnels to another world. Keir's dad changed his name from Geraint to Clint, became a continuity announcer for local television, took a beating as part of a botched insurance scam, killed himself. After his dad died, Keir carried on with his life, went to school every day, opened a coffee shop, found God, studied to become a doctor, moved to Canada.

Does Keir still like Ninja Turtles, Hill thinks.

Felt turned on watching Keir's sister sit on Keir's face that time, Hill thinks.

Clint, fuck, what an idiot, Hill thinks.

Hill looks straight ahead. The water looks calm, grey. The water looks cold, grey. Hill used to canoe in this water. The canoe instructor could never remember his name and Hill didn't like doing barrel rolls. Hill's mother said he could stop going to canoe club if he wanted and try something else instead. Instead of canoeing, Hill went on long bike rides with his friend Max. Max was a blond boy with a French dad called Guy. Guy would take them to the pub and leave them in the large games room at the back whilst he drank in the lounge bar. The room had Pacman and Paperboy and a few other old arcade machines, a pool table, and a large stack of chairs piled up in the corner. Guy wore an oversized blue cable-knit sweater, drank Stella, and set fire to his wedding suit in the garden one evening.

Litany of fathers, Hill thinks.

Hill looks straight ahead.

The path to the side of the fields and down towards the shore is well maintained. People use this path when they're out walking. Some people walk alone, some in couples or small groups, some with dogs. They can walk down towards the shore and stand there looking at the water or the mountains or the bridge to the left of them or the bridge to the right of them. If it's summer and the weather is nice it will be a glorious experience and they can feel lucky to live in such a beautiful place. If it's winter and the weather is bad it will seem like an awful experience and feel oppressive and miserable.

Hill looks straight ahead and recalls a conversation with Trudy where she said that it was up to him how he reacted to different situations, that there wasn't a preordained outcome or fixed emotion he was going to experience.

Would feel happy here in the winter, Hill thinks.

Would enjoy the rain here, Hill thinks.

Nothing is bad, everything is okay, Hill thinks.

Transcend emotions, Hill thinks.

Be productive, Hill thinks.

Feel what you choose to feel, Hill thinks.

Make things, Hill thinks.

Don't do anything you don't like doing, Hill thinks.

Did Clint care; did Guy care; Did McCarthy care, Hill thinks.

People are funny, Hill thinks.

Zen nihilism, Hill thinks.

If I wanted to feel happy I would feel happy by now, Hill thinks.

If I wanted to feel sad I would feel sad by now, Hill thinks.

Try to exist the best you can, Hill thinks.

Stop overreacting, Hill thinks.

Exist quietly, Hill thinks.

Observations only, Hill thinks.

Less open tabs, Hill thinks.

Be more open, Hill thinks.

Enjoy moments, Hill thinks.

Thank you, Jack, Hill thinks.

Did Lucy care, Hill thinks.

Lucy cared, Hill thinks.

Snow, mountain, shore, water, shore, field, path, snow, mountain, Hill thinks.

Sweating, Hill thinks.

Snow, mountain, shore, water, shore, field, path, snow, mountain, Hill thinks.

In this moment, Hill thinks.

I'm like Roger, I'm not like Roger, Hill thinks.

Roger, Hill thinks.

I'm like Hill, I'm not like Hill, Hill thinks.

Roger, Hill thinks.

What do pain and death smell like, Hill thinks.

Only today, only this moment, Hill thinks.

Snow, mountain, shore, water, shore, field, path, snow, mountain, Hill thinks.

Sweating, Hill thinks.

Snow, mountain, shore, water, shore, field, path, snow, mountain, Hill thinks.

Is the temperature okay, Hill thinks.

Hill turns the volume down on the radio.

Is the temperature okay, Hill says.

Thank you for bringing me here, Hill, Roger says. The temperature is fine.

Acknowledgements

Diolch o galon: Amy Roberts, Bibi Buddug, Iola Gal; Carys Roberts; Susie Wildsmith; Richard Davies; Tom Bullough; Adam Christopher Smith; Bill Broady; Amy Lloyd; Rhys Thomas; Jen Giddings; Dr Richard Xavier; Mr West; all ultras

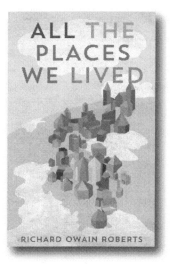

All The Places We Lived

Richard Owain Roberts
ISBN 978-1-910409-65-7
£8.99 • Paperback

'The Welsh David Foster Wallace' –
Srdan Srdic

'... the satirical style of Brett Easton
Ellis ... *Revolutionary Road* by
Richard Yates ... but more than
anything, read it if you like great
fiction' – Wales Arts Review

Things that Make the Heart Beat Faster

João Morais
ISBN 978-1-912109-01-2
£9.00 • Paperback

'love letters to a Cardiff few people
from outside the city will ever
really know, except perhaps
through Morais' fierce eye and
incisive ear for detail. To read him
is to feel you've been granted
access to a kaleidoscopic riot of a
place where you wouldn't
ordinarily be allowed.'
– Rachel Trezise

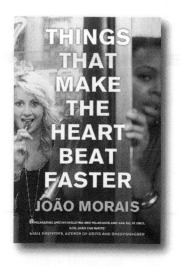

PARTHIAN   Fiction

The Levels

Helen Pendry
ISBN 978-1-912109-40-1
£8.99 • Paperback

'...an important new literary voice.'
– Wales Arts Review

Leading to Texas-2

Aled Smith
ISBN 978-1-912109-11-1
£8.99 • Paperback

'Aled Smith has mixed a dark and
twisted filmic cocktail.'
– Des Barry

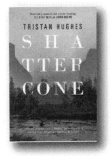

Shattercone

Tristan Hughes
ISBN 978-1-912681-47-1
£8.99 • Paperback

'Beautifully nuanced and
utterly touching'
– *The Daily Mail* on *Hummingbird*

The Blue Tent

Richard Gwyn
ISBN 978-1-912681-28-0
£10 • Paperback

'One of the most satisfying, engrossing and
perfectly realised novels of the year.'
– *The Western Mail*